Book One of

The Sanguine Sorrow

Trilogy

the
Sentimental Dead
Ravven White
Curious Corvid Publishing

For Mep

who always asked after a book I didn't believe
would ever be finished

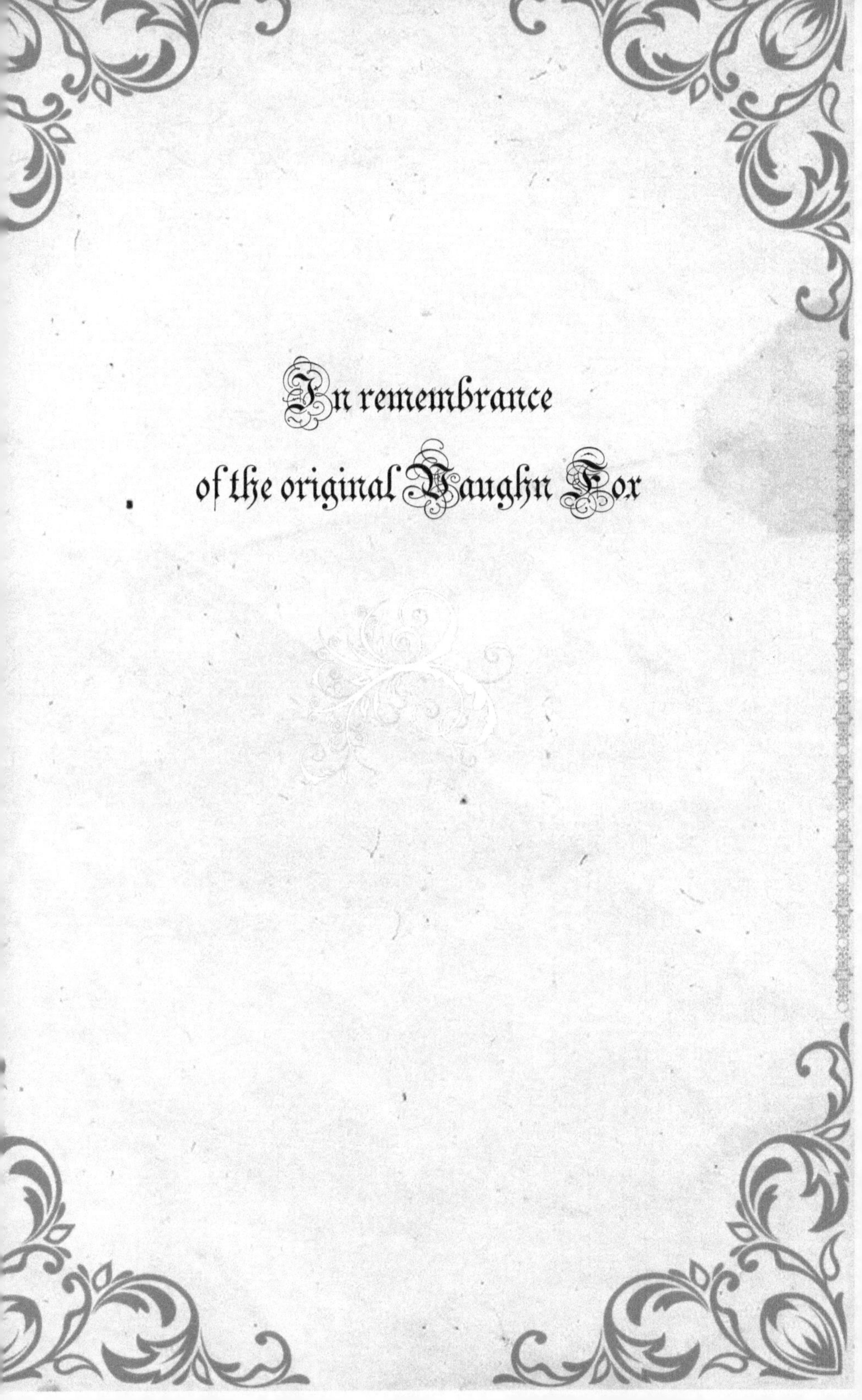

In remembrance
of the original Vaughn Fox

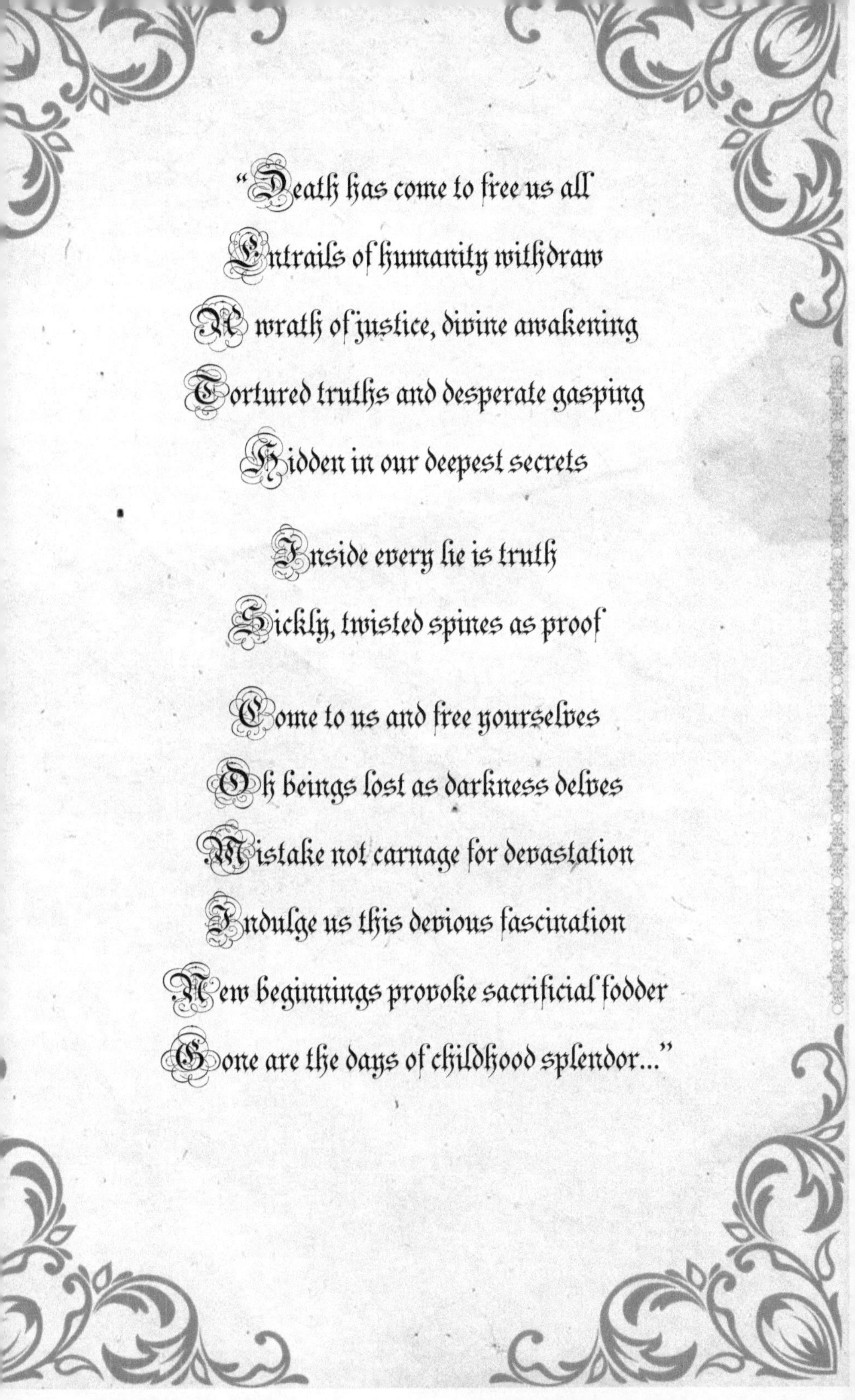

"Death has come to free us all

Entrails of humanity withdraw

A wrath of justice, divine awakening

Tortured truths and desperate gasping

Hidden in our deepest secrets

Inside every lie is truth

Sickly, twisted spines as proof

Come to us and free yourselves

Of beings lost as darkness delves

Mistake not carnage for devastation

Indulge us this devious fascination

New beginnings provoke sacrificial fodder

Gone are the days of childhood splendor..."

Chapter One

"And a great darkness shall come from within

It will cover the sins both ancient and new..."

In The Beginning

Smoke lingered in the air, wafting from a smoldering cigarette. A light fog had rolled in, playfully dancing with the fumes down the darkened street. Streetlamps flickered, casting shadows across the worn brick road. A moonless night emphasized the deep darkness, the streets existing in complete silence. Emptiness.

A solitary figure leaned against a lamppost, deliberating over the cigarette. His ashen blond hair fell over his face where two crystal-blue eyes peered from beneath frowning eyebrows. He brought the cigarette to his lips, coolly, before taking a drag. He inhaled smoothly, a slight smirk spreading across his thin lips. The smirk disappeared and his narrow eyes widened as he cringed and coughed, spitting the cigarette out.

"I told you to stop trying to look cool," a man with a dark and deep voice called out. "Not only do you look ridiculous, but you're wasting a beautiful thing!"

"What the hell, Ash?!" the gagging smoker responded. He bent forward, leaning on his knees as he retched. "Why did I think this was a good idea?"

"Because you're dumb," Ash replied. "Maybe if you weren't so dumb, I wouldn't have to be around so much!" A man approached from the shadows and took the cigarette, inhaling deeply before settling into a ghostly smile.

"I'm not dumb! Why are you always getting on my case?" Emile yelled. "And why do you always show up at inopportune moments? It's like you lie in wait, watching, you creep!"

"Calm down," Ash replied, flicking the butt down the street. "You're always overreacting. If you didn't like it in The Before, you certainly won't like it now." His white teeth flashed against his tan skin, making the scar across his left cheek less sinister. Even with pointed teeth, Ash's smile was warm and welcoming and lightened his typical moody demeanor.

"Whatever," Emile replied, sweeping his hair away from his eyes. He glared at Ash, who had lit another cigarette and was peacefully puffing away. Dammit, why did he always look so cool? With his stupid trench coat, scars, and silky black hair. Emile rolled his eyes and swallowed his sarcastic response. You couldn't argue with Ash and win. Emile had known him long enough to know that. Known him in The Before and The After.

The streetlights flashed off the brass buttons on Ash's long blue coat as he briskly turned and began walking down the street. The cigarette hung playfully from his lips as he strode, his hands in his pockets. Something glinted in his eye as he thoughtfully rolled the cigarette from one corner of his mouth to the other.

"Are you coming or are you going to stay and pout?" he called over his shoulder.

"Who's pouting? I don't know why you even smoke those things anyway." Emile pushed himself off the lamppost. "It's not like you get anything from it anymore. There's not even a risk to smoking them!" Emile ran to catch up to his friend.

"True," Ash responded. "I guess I just like the taste."

"Disgusting."

"I'm sorry, what were you doing just a few minutes ago?" Ash grinned at Emile, puffing a heavy cloud in his direction.

Emile continued walking, his arms folded across his chest. He would not give in. He would not.

"Maybe it's the memories. Or what I wish I had," Ash said quietly, handing the ember butt to his friend before walking toward a building.

"Dad hated that you smoked. Mom hated it more. But I always admired it. A rough city boy full of adventure and darkness, puffing on your cigarettes like a man of mystery instead of an awkward fifteen-year-old boy." Emile grimaced. "It just wasn't fair that you had all the rugged good looks *and* a mysterious backstory."

Ash chuckled. "Don't count yourself out, Emile. You're scrappy and smart! Any being would be lucky to bed you, friend you, or marry you." He winked and walked into a dilapidated building sitting just far enough off the road you almost missed it. The whole town was a bit old and crumbling, leftover remnants of a bygone era. Before the war, before the chaos. Before Emile found himself where he currently was.

He held the butt as it burned down to his fingers, long white fingers that began to smolder and smoke as his flesh turned pink. He waited for the burn to turn to pain and then sighed when it didn't. He let go and watched the butt extinguish in a murky puddle. The waters rippled, and for a moment, Emile allowed himself to ripple within, reaching for lost fragments of the past. When fires scorched skin and sunlight merely warmed it, when food was a necessity not a pleasure, when life . . . was life.

He scratched his face and saw that the burns were almost completely gone. He watched as the skin grafted and wove itself across his thumb until it was perfect and smooth once again. It made him uncomfortable that it disappeared that easily, as if nothing had happened in the first place. When Emile had been fresh bitten, he'd experimented on various parts of his body to see just how well his new body worked. He had been disappointed to find out that everything always healed.

Behind him, a door swung open and slammed, disturbing his reverie. Drunken beings staggered through the doorway as he turned to view them. They were like Emile, but not. Sickly looking creatures with sunken eyes and black veins peeking through white flesh. Maybe they had once been human. Maybe they had once been beautiful. Now, they were neither.

"Come on, baby, we got this just for you." Three females hung on the body of a young man, hands groping and prodding, tongues flicking between pointed teeth. He stumbled forward as greedy hands held him steady.

"Open your mouth!" One of the girls forcefully grabbed the young man's head, forcing it back and pouring the contents of a flask of liquid down his throat. He began choking, liquid mixed with blood spraying across the road, his breath caught in his lungs. He gasped frantically as though he was drowning and attempted to swallow and catch his breath.

"Swallow it, you little punk!" one of the girls screamed at his face.

"Swallow it, sweet boy, swallow," cooed another, stroking his hair thoughtfully. "Swallow so we can all enjoy paradise."

The other female stood behind him, her sickly arms wrapped around his slender body. She nuzzled his neck and licked at him, hungrily.

Emile ran over, pushing himself between the bloodthirsty creatures and the choking boy. He pushed the young lad forward, slapping his back, attempting to protect him from the rabid women.

"Spit it out!" he demanded. "Spit it out, and I'll help you get out of here."

"Who do you think you are?" spat one of the females, her teeth flashing, ready for a fight. The other two flanked her, hissing and twitching. Blood deprived vampires weren't ones to be messed with. The black veins and chaotic movements meant they were in a weakened state but not helpless.

Emile narrowed his eyes. "None of your goddamn business. Why don't you leave this poor kid alone? He clearly doesn't want your 'paradise.' Look at him, he can barely breathe!"

"You know we can't get high without him!" one of them whined.

"You know that it's illegal here!" Emile retorted.

"Not illegal, just . . . frowned upon. Look around you, this is no golden city. Nobody cares what happens in places like this. Why should you?"

"I can take you into containment, I'm a hunter in Squall."

"Go ahead, take us in. They won't do anything. You think the local chapter has time for some hungry vamps?"

Emile knew she was right. Even if he could take them in, he knew that the stationed company didn't have the time or the care for some wayward druggies. But if the boy wasn't a willing participant . . .

"Be on your way and we'll act like none of this happened," countered the leading female.

Emile narrowed his eyes, slashing the air between him and the girls. "Stay back."

"He's ours!"

They lunged toward Emile, who flashed his fangs and growled, his teeth glinting, his body heaving with anger. "I said, stay back. Look at you pathetic pieces of shit. You can barely stand. You think you can take me? Think twice."

The girls backed off, snarling and hissing. Emile knew they were reassessing the situation. Whatever he did next would have to be fast and precise. Beside Emile, the boy stood up and weakly took a step forward. His hands shook, and as he raised his eyes to Emile, he smiled a sad, twisted smile.

"Thanks," he whispered, "but I don't need your help."

Grabbing the flask from his companions, he drank. He gulped desperately, greedily, his hands shaking uncontrollably as he consumed every last drop of liquid. The empty flask fell to the ground, clanging against the brick street as he walked forward, arms spread open.

"Come now," he said, tilting his head back. "Feast on me!"

The girls flocked to him, licking and kissing his neck before sinking their fangs into his flesh. They drank hungrily, moaning as they slurped and sucked down his neck and arms, fresh wounds marbling his skin. He stayed still as they held him, his eyes glazed over and his face still holding that sad, twisted smile. After a moment, they collapsed onto the ground in a heap, the females still lapping at the dripping wounds and giggling drunkenly. Leaning over the broken man, they began to lick the blood off each other's fingers and skin. Blood mixed with dirt and sweat and who knows what, festering on their blighted bodies. *Blights.* That was what they were—that was what they would become.

Emile gave one last look of disgust before turning his back and facing the building Ash had disappeared into. There was nothing he could do now. The human had made his choice.

"Bye-bye, savior boy. Guess you'll need to find someone else to save," taunted the leader before bursting out into a crazed laugh.

Emile's fists clenched, drawing blood from his palms. "Vamps like you are filth," he said quietly over his shoulder. "Got a second chance at life and all you do is chase your next high. You should have just stayed dead."

The girls, enraptured in blood, ignored him as he placed his hand on the door. He heard them stand and drag the unconscious man back into the building they had burst from. He paused only for a moment before taking a breath and walking inside.

"Welcome to the Sentimental Dead! Can I get you a drink?"

If there were ever magic left in the world, it would surely be found here, at the Sentimental Dead. Emile already felt the stress and anger fading from him as the quiet darkness and warmth of the bar enveloped his entire being, and he shrugged off the feasting he knew was happening next door. He locked eyes with Morgan, the attending barkeep, and dusted off his shirt.

"Oh hey, Morgan. I didn't know you were working tonight."

The bartender shrugged, looking unimpressed, and continued polishing a glass. "What can I get you?"

"Well, I bet anything you make is delicious," Emile replied. Morgan stared at him blankly, still working away on the cocktail glass, which caused Emile to immediately backpedal.

"Delicious because, you know, you're really good at your job. Professionally speaking. As one professional to another—not that I bartend drinks. Not that I wouldn't bartend . . ."

"I'll take this one, Morgan. Why don't you check on our friends down the hall?" a deep voice countered from behind the heavy curtains. The barkeep shrugged again and continued on their way. Emile watched them go, somewhat relieved but keeping a face of disappointment. As with every other person Emile was even remotely attracted to, he just didn't have the confidence or suave conversation to land a date. Or even a drink.

"Emile!" the voice continued. "You're late! Heard you were trying to be a hero, though, so I can't argue with that." From behind the velvet curtains emerged the owner of the Sentimental Dead and one of the last remaining warlocks in the human realm. The golden candle flames glowed across his dark skin, decorated in scars from the war. He towered over the counter, closer to giant than man, two small black horns crowning his short-clipped silver hair. His brown eyes were twinkling with amusement.

"Sean, it's always good to see you, even when you interrupt my inspired conversations with your lovely barkeeps."

Sean raised an eyebrow. "*Inspired* is the word you chose to go with today? Are you sure that's an accurate choice? We all know how these conversations go." Sean winked.

Emile sighed. "You're as irritating as Ash sometimes, you know? I'll take a Heart Beater, please. Light on the vitamin D. Also, how did you know what I was doing from all the way in here?"

Sean chuckled and gestured down the bar to a back room half-cloaked in velvet. "As if anything can happen around here without me knowing. Heart Beater coming right up. Your friends are over in the corner, as usual."

"Thank you, Sean."

The bartender turned and deftly mixed together Emile's drink. Few beings were gifted with the knowledge of whom Sean was—a relic from the days of magic. A warlock who grew tired of the battlefield after the purging in the war and retired, opting for a simple life. A quiet life. A dignified life. And that was why this place was so special. Emile leaned on the counter, gazing across the room.

The Sentimental Dead was the bar for those once human who missed their humanity and for those who no longer had a place in humanity. Each drink was a mixture of magic and science, and the Nutrimentum ones were designed to mimic physical and emotional responses that vampires no longer experienced. Thanks to Sean's many gifts and magical influence, not only were the drinks unique and delightful, but Sean also kept a magical barrier around the building, making it look ordinary from the outside and causing most beings to turn a blind eye. Entrance to the Sentimental Dead was by invite only, making it a haven for nonhuman creatures. And gods was it luxurious. Crushed black and purple velvet tapestries, gilded banisters and woodwork, black roses and dim lights, a perfect place to brood and reminisce.

"Emile!" a high-pitched voice rang out. "Over here, come and join us!"

Across the bar to the right, tucked in a corner, sat Ash and two other vamps. A young, bouncy girl with golden curls and a corset of knives waved at Emile. Emile grabbed his drink and headed over, soulful jazz music floating after him from an old record player.

"Emile, where have you been? Ash said you were right behind him?" the girl asked playfully, pulling on a curl.

"I got held up by some druggies. Sick bastards. They should stay in Lordestowne where they belong," Emile explained angrily as he sat down beside Ash.

"Why do you care?" Ash asked, a new cigarette hanging from his lips as he casually polished his silver revolver.

"Because he has a savior complex," a sultry voice interjected.

"Good evening, Annora," Emile greeted, attempting to turn on the charm. "Can I just say, you are looking remarkably lovely this evening? Respectfully. Of course." he coughed awkwardly.

At the end of the table a dignified, voluptuous beauty sat leaning back in the booth, her long legs stretched across the table. Her pale skin was a stark contrast to the black lace and velvet that delicately displayed her curves. Between her thigh-high boots, scooping blouse, and black wavy hair pinned at the sides, she was a picture of elegance and sex. To Emile, she was a goddess—unattainable but impossible to ignore. She was a bloodthirsty type of radiance while also somehow a safe space for Emile to express himself. He knew he wasn't Annora's type so there was never any fear of her returning his compliments.

"What about me?" implored a whiny voice.

"Nyx, you know you always look good," Emile replied, brushing her off.

"Stop pouting, Violetta," Ash interjected. "It's ruining your face."

She stuck her tongue out and shuffled in her seat beside Annora. Violetta Nyx. Her blond curls tickled her cleavage as she stroked her new corset. Her manicured nails clicked as they stroked down the shiny handles hosting a variety of dangerous knives.

"Look at my new getup," she said. "It can hold twice as many knives, and it's my favorite colors: purple, black, and lace."

"Lace isn't a color," Ash replied. "But you do look nice. Didn't think you could push your tits up any more, but I guess I was wrong." he leaned back in his chair and grinned devilishly.

"This is why you're lonely and will always be lonely and will die alone!" Violetta yelled. "Besides, I just want to look good for all the handsome boys." She pulled out a mirror and touched up her dark purple lipstick before waving with a coy smile at the male vamps lounging at the bar. Several of them winked or waved back until they locked eyes with Ash who had turned to view Violetta's audience.

Annora rolled her eyes and watched, amused. She looked between Ash and Violetta before raising an eyebrow to Emile. Without moving her lips, she asked, *"Who will win this time?"*

Emile figured it was about fifty-fifty as Violetta and Ash both had viper-like attitudes and insufferable stubbornness.

"Such a tease." Ash tsked, turning back around. "Doesn't it shame you at all to lead on the poor bastards?"

"Not at all," she replied coolly, snapping open one of her switchblades. "They can look all they want. They just can't touch." She smiled wickedly. "It's a shame when they do."

"Leaving bloody stumps everywhere is no doubt their biggest turn-on."

Violetta smirked and cocked her head, a slightly crazed look overtaking her features. Emile scooched back from the table and away from Ash, but Ash made no move and sat with his arms crossed, smiling back. Emile always felt a little uncomfortable when Ash and Violetta went back and forth but he knew that Ash reveled in it.

"Don't touch what isn't yours and there won't be a problem," she crooned.

"Any person that messes with you, Violetta, has it coming," Ash replied, raising his glass and tipping his head in respect.

Violetta smiled and settled into her chair, idly tracing the tip of her switchblade into the wooden table, marring the smooth surface. She and Ash held eye contact for a bit before breaking apart.

"Where is Foxxe?" Emile coughed, breaking the tension.

"Apparently late," replied a voice behind him. "Forgive me. Annora, Violetta, you look lovely this evening. Excuse me while I retrieve my drink from the bar."

"And our company is complete," Annora said quietly, sipping her drink. She looked over at Emile. *"I think Violetta took this one home."*

Emile drew a slight smile as he tilted his head and conceded, *"It certainly appears that way."*

Foxxe pulled up a chair to the end of the booth and pulled out a folded piece of paper. "Here are some new reports of a blight in the town over. Two humans are dead, three are wounded." Foxxe slid the papers over for the crew to review. "Came out of nowhere, without any warnings. One of the other companies took it out, but they can't figure out where it came from."

Ash and Emile glanced at each other.

"Have you heard anything from the elites about these sudden cases?" Emile asked.

"Just murmurs. Everyone is very hush-hush about it," Foxxe replied, sipping on his brandy. "Elites don't even trust elites, and they certainly don't trust turned." He paused for a moment, swirling his drink. "My sources do say, however, that something is happening in their infrastructure. I just don't know if it's related to the blight or if it's politics. There's been talk of some . . . unconventional experimentation between humans and vampires for a possible cure."

"*Unconventional*," Ash replied. "As if our existence was conventional to begin with."

"But I thought the treaty forbade these kinds of things!" Emile interjected. "It's the whole point of what we do. Work with humans to get the supply we need and contribute to society and science. Not treat them like cattle. Any vampire at any time can get the blood they need if they just follow procedure."

"It wouldn't be so bad if we could feed off all blood types," Annora interjected. "But that's just not the case. And following procedures doesn't always get you what you need."

Emile had grown very familiar with the ways of the vampire world. He'd watched vampires succumb to the blight purely because they couldn't get the blood type they needed. Humans still had the upper hand and their strained coexistence didn't always lend itself towards kindness. Sometimes vampires just had to wait and make do. To try and balance the blood needs, scientists invented Nutrimentum: a blend of synthetic and natural blood to help water down the blood lines. As progressive as it was, it didn't agree with all vampires. Plus, consuming it required more continuous feedings as the energy it supplied was not as long-lasting as pure blood. History was not kind when it came to vampires and humans intermingled and Elites had always done what they must to survive, regardless of the harm inflicted.

"The elites are just a bunch of bastards," Violetta remarked. "No offense, Annora. And Foxxe."

"None taken," Annora replied, amused.

"Whatever the case," Foxxe continued. "There are more and more blights showing up across the country. Nobody knows where they are coming from. There's always going to be rogue vamps, and with the lingering hostile climate left by the war, not every human has accepted our existence. Times are still hard. But between the good nature fostered by companies like ours as well as the legislature linking vamps with blood banks, there shouldn't be as many blights as there have been. It is concerning. Between our company and those in the other districts, we've been able to keep close tabs on all possible blights. And since we can track blight progression better than humans can, there's no explanation for why they are occurring so spontaneously."

"These blights are just going to piss off the elites even more," Ash pointed out. "They're going to use it to justify whatever messed-up thing they are planning. Or doing."

"Maybe someone should remind the ever-powerful elites that they can't change the laws of nature. I've a mind to just go down there myself and have it out with the lord of the clan!" Emile slammed his fist on the table.

"May I remind you, Emile," Foxxe interjected over his glass, "elites are not to be trifled with. I know you have feelings about Elites in general and while they are valid, they should not cloud your judgment in action or word."

Emile reluctantly agreed. He knew the history and the stories. The stories of the original vampires, first born with a unique genetic mutation. Wild, ravenous beings that were believed to be born of sin and corruption. Rejected by their human families, elites created their own dominion in the dark. Everyone knew the stories of bloodsucking creatures that fed on babies and lured innocent maidens to their doom. In the beginning, vampires remained few and far between as they themselves were unable to reproduce. They only began amassing numbers after a blood drinking gone wrong—when the human awoke with vampiric attributes. The turned.

From there, elites bolstered their numbers and began creating cities flooded with freshly created turned. Some were willing. Some were not. But once you became a creature of the night, there was no place for you in the human realm. Survival brought them together. But the turned had a unique twist to their rebirth—a sleeping corruption in their DNA. Turned required blood, with the need unique to each one. Some turned thrived on B or A blends, some only O types. And corrupted blood—that was a whole other story. Turned vamps who didn't get the nutrients they needed would begin a slow deterioration. A slow death. A gruesome death.

Emile looked down into his cup, the contents slightly bubbling. He drank it slowly, enjoying the tingling sensation as it ran down his throat. The Heart Beater was his favorite drink. It smelled faintly of blackberries and tasted like sweet cream and sugar. It reminded him of his mother's homemade pies. The crust golden and crumbling and topped in decadent hand-whipped cream. He closed his eyes and placed his hand on his chest. For a few moments he could feel a faint rhythm, as though his heart had started beating faster again. He smiled faintly.

His heart still beat, but not how it once did. That's what being turned did to you. Maybe a vampire's body was a sculpted evolutionary step—streamlined energy usage, increased endurance and mobility, longer life, and sharper sense, but there was a dark side to this life. The blighted side when vampires who did not get the blood they needed, or overdosed on different or corrupted types, sped up the awakening of the blight mutation. Skin would fall from their bones, as rotting and festering wounds turning them into decaying corpses of hunger that would devour as much human flesh as they could to try and regenerate. But it never worked, and they would die an agonizing death as a twisted, broken monster.

"I knew a guy who couldn't drink B because it gave him a horrible rash, everywhere. *Everywhere,*" Violetta said, bringing Emile back to the conversation. "I knew another guy that couldn't drink A because it gave him horrible cramps and stomach spasms."

"So, it gave him the shits is what you're saying?" Ash replied.

"Thank you for that," she retorted. "Yes, it gave him the shits."

"I guess there are some things even vamps can't escape from," he replied.

"Please stay on topic," Foxxe interjected. "The blight is gone, but I want someone to go scout the area, talk to the locals, and see if anything was missed."

"I think Violetta and I can handle this one," Annora said. "Let the women take care of things."

"What if you need a big strong man to save you?" Emile asked, flexing his biceps.

"Then I'll be sure to call for one," Annora replied smoothly. "But it's highly unlikely. We'll leave first thing in the morning."

Emile relaxed in his chair and pondered the evening's events. Foxxe gathered up the papers and folded them, tucking them back into his coat. A cream-colored envelope stamped with an official seal fell from the bunch. Foxxe frowned and snatched it up quickly, resecuring it.

"That looked important," commented Emile.

"Just more people who anticipate my assistance," Foxxe replied tiredly. "Everyone has an agenda these days. I've been so busy working with the other districts to try and decipher the rise in blights, I don't have much time for anything else. The war ended fifty years ago and sometimes it feels like just yesterday, fighting to secure a place in this world, trying to fix all the things that have gone wrong. Righting injustices and attempting peace. And now this. It doesn't help that blight transformation is so unpredictable. One turned vamp can indulge in corrupted blood for decades and never a sign. Another can do it for a few years and then begin the mutation. But either way, it's a long, drawn-out process. You don't just get a blight overnight."

"Wiping out the blights is all well and good," Ash interjected, "but what are we going to do if the elites really are kidnapping humans and experimenting on them?"

"Obviously we'd fight them!" Emile replied.

"Oh yes because our band is enough to take on the power of the elites," Ash retorted. Emile sighed. Squall was a private extermination unit hired by the human military, but the coexistence was terribly strained and unpredictable. The same held for the Elites.

"But we can't just sit back and do nothing!" Emile replied, gesturing desperately. "We are the best equipped to deal with the situation. And we have Foxxe and Annora, former elites."

"I'm not saying we shouldn't do something." Ash slammed his fist on the table. "I'm just saying it's going to be really freaking hard, and our company alone is not enough."

Annora shared a knowing look with Foxxe before straightening her shoulders and sipping her drink. Violetta continued to trace her dagger into the dark wooden table, scratching symbols across her corner. Foxxe sipped his drink and swirled the amber liquid thoughtfully.

They sat silently for a moment, contemplating a delicate future. To ignore human abduction was an impossible solution. They had worked hard to establish a friendly network and had proven their loyalty by working with the military to protect and defend the human population. Then there was the rise in blight infestation. The two had to be related.

"What do you think, Foxxe?" Emile asked.

Foxxe lit a cigarette and leaned back in his chair. "Lines have been crossed. And it would seem we've been drawn into a rebellion."

Chapter Two

"Blood shall mix with the past and the present

An omen of those who walk silent among us..."

Ash and Emile exchanged sobered looks. They had not been around for the first war—well before their time. Emile wondered if the war hero resting before him was ready for another bloodbath. Probably not. Foxxe was a celebrated savior—an elite who had rejected the ways of his clan and had fought alongside humans. But vampires and humans weren't the only casualties. Those born with celestial powers, summoners of energy, and shifters had died in masses during the human purges. Many simply vanished and became ghosts of myths and legends. Some, such as the wolfhounds, were collected and contained as weapons by the government. And any born with special gifts simply hid them.

Emile knew that the loss of magical creatures and imprisonment of wolfhounds haunted Foxxe. Foxxe considered it one of his biggest failures. He had been an influential leader in bringing peace, but not all creatures were afforded the luxury of a happy ending. Vampires would live among the population, quietly. They would register with the government and live in designated cities, and they would assist in protection and defense in exchange for cooperative blood banks and supply depots. But time could not erase the hurts inflicted by both sides. Humans continued to remember vampires as the bloodthirsty savages that preyed on innocents and lived among the shadows.

The world Emile knew was not a beautiful one. Drastic measures taken by both sides during the war had devastated economies and brought both countries and governments to their knees. Entire villages and cities had been decimated, and the body count had been astronomical. It had been a war unlike any other and had left the world broken, a fraction of a shadow of what it had once been. Technology had come to a stand still. Resources were few and far between. The earth was quiet as people communicated through patched together receivers, survived on generators, and adapted to a post-apocalyptic society.

"If I am right and we are being drawn into this fight, it's important we surround ourselves with loyal allies who share a vision of peace and prosperity. Emile, after your patrol with Violetta I want you to go to City Salvatore and talk to the new director about building a blood bank there. He shows a lot of promise."

"Wait, you want me to be a diplomat?" Emile asked incredulously. "I have no interest in going into a human city. Send Annora. She's far more diplomatic and . . . fancy," he ended desperately.

"You've been hiding for ten years," Foxxe said. "That's long enough. Go there and represent Squall. I know you are more than capable. And no, Ash can't go with you." He anticipated Emile's next question. "He has some rogues to hunt." Foxxe handed Emile a packet of papers. "When I was at the local chapter I sent him a message that you'd be arriving in my place. Since there's no reception here, and it's so broken along the way, you'll have to announce your arrival at the capitol gate. These papers should keep you from any trouble."

Emile took them doubtfully and looked them over with Ash.

"Goodnight, boys," Foxxe said quietly, picking up his drink. "I'll see you tomorrow."

"Goodnight, Foxxe," they replied together. But they knew Foxxe wasn't going home. On the other far side of the bar sat a piano, and many a night when the mood was melancholy, Foxxe would make his way to the ivory keys and would soon be lost in reverie. Within moments, they heard the keys softly twinkling and a delicate, haunting tune floated back where they sat.

"Well boys, we are heading out also," Annora said. "We'll be back sometime tomorrow or the day after."

"Try not to miss us too much," Violetta said, blowing a kiss on her way out. Ash jokingly caught it as they said goodbye to their companions. The bar slowly emptied, but Ash and Emile lingered, listening to the soft piano keys. Emile found it oddly comforting.

"He certainly is a classic," Ash took a drag on his cigarette. "Only one I know that appreciates piano music from a bygone era."

"I wonder when he learned to play," Emile mused.

"I heard it was when he met a girl."

"Not just a girl," interrupted a voice. Sean stepped out from behind the velvet drapes. "*The* girl. When Vaughn was a young blood making his name in the war."

"I don't think we know this story," Ash replied.

Sean smiled softly. "He fell in love with a beautiful human girl named Liliana who worked as a nurse on the battlefields. Theirs was a doomed love though, and Vaughn wrestled with the line drawn between them of human and vampire. But however doomed, it was real, and together they decided to let it live and grow. It was a nice reprieve in the midst of chaos. Watching Foxxe pick a flower for his beloved before entering the war tents." Sean sighed and wiped the table, his striking dark face contemplative.

"And what happened to Liliana?" asked Emile.

Sean smiled sadly. "She died. She became ill and withered away from fevers and pain. Vaughn offered to turn her, but she said that it was not her destiny and she would see him again in the next life. She changed Foxxe. She made him kinder and softer and even in death she managed to make him a better person."

"Did Vaughn learn to play for Liliana?"

"No. He learned because of Liliana. Because she made his heart sing. When he plays, I think it is the closest thing he has to holding her again."

Sean glanced at the table where the pair sat. "Tell Violetta she owes me a new table for scratching this one up. I swear that girl and her knives."

"Sean?" Emile asked. "If things escalate in our world, would you return to battle? Would you take up arms?"

Ash looked up at him, curious.

"Of course," Sean replied. "And I'd fight on the same side as before. For people like Vaughn. And for people like Liliana. For her relationship with Foxxe. It defied societal norms and laws and showed that there can be peace and restoration. There could be hope."

"She sounded lovely."

"Oh, she was. It didn't matter to her what you were as long as you were kind. Some of us are born into this life scraping and fighting to be good. Liliana was just born good. And I'll fight for that every day."

Sean continued on his way, and Ash and Emile sat and listened to the soft tunes from the piano. Melancholic but laced in love. In longing. In hope. As they left the building, Foxxe's eyes were closed, his brandy atop the piano, his hands delicately dancing. Lost in memories. Looking so . . . human. Emile looked away as though invading a private moment. And he wondered at the idea of a born monster becoming so human.

Chapter Three

"For beware we must be of the beasts
Harbingers of destruction and madness..."

The Blade That Bends

It was another brisk night. High winds howled and licked at the corners of Emile's jet black leather jacket. He preferred solely wearing his leather vest, deftly pocketed with knives, gadgets, and his current favorite book. But tonight was cold even for a vampire, and it was better not to waste any energy healing frostbitten skin. It had been nearly ten years since he'd been turned, and he was still learning bits and pieces on how this new life worked. Not that he enjoyed it.

In fact, in the beginning he'd been downright resistant. Lucky for him, Ash had been there. Ash had been a vampire for a few years before Emile was fresh bitten, and he had already experimented with different survival techniques. Surviving on animals, trying different synthetics, feeding on donors. As Emile went through his change, Ash stayed beside him, caring for him and encouraging him to feed. But Emile didn't want to. He wanted to waste away. He wasn't brave enough to face this new life like Ash did. Ash had always been braver than Emile, even in The Before.

After Ash had been turned, he'd been left to die on the streets of Lordestowne. He'd dragged himself out of the city, determined not to die in that hell of a place, and that was how Emile's father had found him. Half-dead by the side of the road and still trying to survive. For a while, Emile hadn't known Ash was a turned vampire. His parents had told him a very glossed-over version of Ash's story: that Ash's family had abandoned him and that he was sick and needed to recover. He looked like a sickly thing, pale and skinny with dark circles under dark eyes. Emile had been fascinated by this mysterious boy from Lordestowne—a place Emile had been told was full of monsters and destruction. A place good men never went for they would never return. Ash was fifteen when he showed up—only a year older than Emile—and Emile was excited to have someone his own age on the farm. His only sibling was his sister Charlotte, and she had just been a baby at the time.

Emile remembered those early days when Ash was adjusting to his new life. He had been quiet and reserved, keeping mostly to himself whether he was working or not. Emile's father had crafted a room in the barn so he could have his own space and privacy. Ash hadn't accepted the offer of the spare bedroom, citing that his natural sleep cycle and activities would disturb the home. Emile had zealously welcomed Ash, inviting him to participate in a host of activities, but Ash just stared sullenly ahead and didn't show any inclination or interest.

Emile's parents told him Ash needed space and time. But the months started to pass, and Ash began to work more and more on the farm, in the fields planting, or in the barns tinkering with old equipment. Emile found it strange that Ash spent most of the mornings and afternoons working away in barns and saving field work for dusk and nighttime or for overcast days when the sun didn't shine quite as much. In fact, there had been many things that caused Emile to question their new guest—that he never joined them for dinner and never seemed to eat. He never talked, he never smiled.

Once, Emile had stumbled on Nutrimentum after his father had brought some home. He'd never before seen the long tubes filled with frothy red liquid. Out of curiosity, he had popped open the top for a better look, his nose wrinkling at the pungent odor.

"What is this?" he asked his mom as she entered the kitchen.

"What are you doing with that?" She had frowned, grabbing up the tube. She paused and then replied, "This is for Ash. He . . . needs a special diet. Because of some things he went through."

"It smells disgusting. What happened to him to make him have to drink that nasty stuff?"

"It's not my story to tell," his mom replied, putting it away. "It's Ash's."

Emile had read plenty of books on monsters and magic, and he'd heard real-life stories at community campfires. Stories recounting the days before the war, of creatures that lurked in the darkness, witches that could transform you into a hideous beast, and fairies that cursed healthy crops for overtaking their fields of wildflowers. Emile's parents tried to shush such stories, countering that not everything was as it seemed, but Emile thought they were only trying to protect him and his sister. So, he watched Ash. And he waited. He waited for the monster to come out of the boy, for the transformation of sulking teen to ravenous beast. But the months passed, and the only wicked thing to come from Emile's watch was the realization that Ash was a chain-smoking, brooding, boring boy.

And then the day finally came that Emile had enough of waiting. He'd rounded the barn Ash was staying in and found him staring down a rabbit. Ash was crouched as if ready to pounce, his eyes wild and focused. A grin had spread across his face, and Emile could see two pointed fangs glinting in the fading light. Faster than Emile had ever seen, Ash suddenly sprinted and snatched the rabbit before it had completed its circle to run. He stood triumphant, the furry creature wriggling in his hands. And then Ash looked up and saw Emile. The smile slowly disappeared, and Ash dropped his hands to his side, letting the rabbit go. The boys stood silently for a moment, surveying each other.

"What do you want?" Ash asked gruffly.

Emile stood silent for a moment. "Can you teach me to catch a rabbit like that?"

Ash raised his eyebrows in surprise. "I don't know. Maybe. Probably not."

At seeing Emile's disappointed face, he added impatiently, "We could try."

"Cool." They both stood awkwardly, unsure of what to do next. "So . . ." Emile began.

"So?" Ash asked, crossing his arms.

"So . . . you're one of the monsters of Lordestowne?"

Ash's face darkened. "Why, are you afraid of me?"

Emile pondered. "Nah. I could take you."

"Oh really?"

"Yeah, all you've done for eight months is brood and work. Not very sinister if you ask me. In fact, it's pretty boring and disappointing."

To Emile's surprise, Ash laughed, and it was a pleasant laugh. Not like a monster at all.

"Maybe I am a monster of Lordestowne. I don't know." His face turned serious. "But I am a turned vamp."

"I had my suspicions," Emile replied nonchalantly.

"Oh, I see. What are you, some kind of detective?"

"I mean, you work at night, you're pale and weird looking, and you drink 'a special diet.' Which by the way smells *disgusting.*"

"Smell equals the taste." Ash grimaced. "It's called Nutrimentum. It's a synthetic blend so I don't have to . . .feed. On humans. It tides me over between blood donations from the blood bank. Also, what do you mean I'm weird looking?"

"I've heard of it. I've read lots of things on vampires. Scary creatures that hunt at night on innocents. Leaders of the rebellion that started the war. And nowadays, bloodthirsty beings that rule cities of corruption."

"Sounds like you've read a lot."

"Yes," Emile said slowly. "Yet here you are hunting rabbits in our backyard. You're not really living up to the hype."

"I have nothing better to do."

Emile paused thoughtfully. "Why don't you come have dinner with us?"

Ash froze, panic leaking into his eyes. "I don't . . . I don't belong . . ."

"There's no reason to keep it a secret anymore. Besides, my father saved you. The least you can do is get to know his family. You're a vampire. That means you're super strong and have special abilities."

"And?"

"And you can use those abilities to protect our family. And you can teach me to protect them too."

"But I thought I was a monster of Lordestowne?"

"If my dad trusts you, so do I," Emile replied. "My dad doesn't make mistakes like that. Neither does my mom. Now come on, it's time to eat." Emile turned and began walking to the house, beckoning Ash to follow. He did so, reluctantly. "Oh, and you're weird looking because of your hair."

"My hair?" Ash asked, rubbing his shorn scalp.

"Yeah, you're long, white, and skinny. Stop shaving your head. You look like a cotton swab."

Ash had begun to protest but shut up as they walked in the house. It was warm and softly lit, Emile's baby sister Charlotte gabbing in her chair. She had smiled and waved bashfully at Ash as they walked in. Emile sat him down and announced to the family that Ash would be dining with them from now on and that he was the family's sworn protector. Emile's father laughed, his mother served Ash his drink, and they all dined together, as a family.

Emile saw the memory in his mind and wished he could freeze it. He wished that he could reach out to them and warn them of what was to come.

"Lost in reverie, are we?" Violetta asked, popping up beside him. "Thinking of a special someone?" she teased.

"Just caught up in some memories," Emile replied, letting the happy glow dissipate.

"Careful with that," Violetta replied. "Memories are a dangerous game. They make you weak and vulnerable."

"In what way? Memories help you remember who you were. Who you loved."

"Sometimes," she answered. "But sometimes we end up trying to be what was and it's just not realistic. We are different people our whole life. Better to let the past die with our old selves."

"My past is dead," he replied bitterly. "It's nothing but death now."

"Then don't stay there."

"Easier said than done."

"Not really."

"Not really? Violetta, my whole life is back there. My family, my . . ."

"No, your life is here. Your life is now. Hello?" she interjected, knocking on Emile's head. "Try and keep up please."

Emile just sighed and rolled his eyes.

"Look at my blade," Violetta said as she whipped out her favorite switchblade. It glinted in the streetlight. "This is my favorite one. Don't tell the other knives, they get jealous. Anyway, what do you see?"

Emile surveyed the weapon. Its black handle inlaid with turquoise flowers and mother-of-pearl swirls led to a sturdy and narrow blade. It was well balanced, durable, and despite having some wear, the blade held its beauty from the obvious care Violetta bestowed it.

"A knife," Emile replied sarcastically.

"Details," Violetta urged.

Emile surveyed the weapon. "I see a blade, well used but still sharp. I see some scratches. Some dents."

"Do you see what made it?"

"What?" he asked, confused.

"Where this blade came from? How it was made? Do you see it?"

"No . . ."

"Exactly." With a flick of the wrist, the blade slipped through her hand and embedded in a broken fence post. "And look at how sharp and beautiful it is," she said, pleased, as she retrieved it. "The world doesn't care what made you or where you came from. It only cares about how it can use you. If you linger too long in the past, then the world will use that against you. So be sharp, be present, be strong. Become your own weapon and you won't be owned by the past or the present."

"I think this is the most inspirational talk we've ever had, Violetta," Emile remarked. "Is this the kind of thing you and Ash talk about on your patrols?"

Violetta walked back with the knife and snapped it shut. "Why? What do you think we talk about?"

Emile swallowed. "Well, I don't know, I just thought . . ."

"Oh, come now Emile, don't backpedal. Say what you mean and stick to it. No wonder you're single. And sad."

"I'm single because I choose to be, just like you. And I'm not *sad*."

"Not at all just like me. I could have anyone I want at any time. You, on the other hand, are just a lot of words."

"I'm good with words!"

"No." Violetta shook her head, "you're really not, which is ironic for someone who likes to read. Let's walk."

Emile fell into place beside her, and they walked in the darkness. Foxxe rotated patrols regularly. He thought it was important that everyone be able to work together one-on-one in case of an emergency. Violetta and Annora were strong together, Ash and Emile were strong together, but split apart they had to learn how to rely on their fellow companions. It was a good strategy, Emile thought. Even if most patrols were spent prowling streets late at night watching for rogues or outlaws. Those nights were extra fun.

"Have you ever had a girlfriend?" Violetta asked.

Emile shook his head.

"Boyfriend?"

Emile blushed and shook his head again.

"Have you ever . . .?" Violetta asked with a vulgar gesture.

Emile blushed again. "No. Never even been kissed."

"Wow," Violetta replied. "Are you just not interested?"

"No, it's not that," Emile replied. "I'm very interested. In many ways. I just. I've never met anyone that I felt compelled to . . .share that with."

"I see," Violetta replied thoughtfully. "Are you afraid of it?"

"No, not in general. I've heard it's quite a lot of fun when done right." He laughed. "I'm not sure if I can have anything like that."

"What do you mean?"

"Listen, I know you and Ash aren't a couple. Technically or whatever."

Violetta raised her eyebrows.

"But you still have this . . . connection, and you both accept each other for who and what you are. But I don't know who I am and I'm afraid . . . I'm afraid by the time I figure it out it will be too late. And if I connect with someone now, maybe they won't . . . love me then. Maybe I'll change. What if I fail them and I'm not who they think I am?"

"Oh my gods, so much drama!" Violetta replied, waving her hands and pretending to faint. "Okay, Emile, so who are you?"

"I'm a fighter. I'm a hunter. I kill things, I drink blood, I live in the dark, and I'm afraid of spiders."

Violetta chuckled. "Okay . . . ?"

"Beyond that I don't know."

"Oh, I see. You think you're no good."

Emile panicked. "I don't mean . . . that doesn't make you . . . we do the same thing but . . ."

"No, it's okay. I'm no good either."

"You're not good?"

"Nah. There's nothing I love more than a good hunt, stalking my prey, making sure they know what's about to happen to them and then capturing them and slicing away while they scream in pain. It's delicious."

Emile remained silent, unsure and a little bit afraid.

"I know what I am," she continued undeterred. "And I make no attempt to hide it. I see no reason to. I do what I do for a good purpose. I help people. I save cities. I defend the innocent. And I love doing it."

They walked for a few minutes, winding through the town. It was empty, desolate, the winds walking with them as if heralding their arrival. Cloaked midnight in more ways than one.

"You don't know how I was turned," Violetta stated.

"No."

"Why have you never asked?"

"I assumed if you wanted me to know, you would tell me."

"When I was a little girl, I dreamed of being the wife of a rich man, living in a house full of pretty things. We would have beautiful children and we would be very, very happy. I dreamed this because my real life was the furthest thing from happy. My father was an abusive alcoholic. When he wasn't passed out from drinking, he was screaming and beating. My mother didn't know how to handle him besides taking his side. So she joined him in the abuse of my brother, Michael, and me. It was just the two of us, me and Michael. And I looked up to him as all little sisters do. But one day he decided he had enough, and he left. He left me there. Alone."

Emile listened silently as they walked.

"Down the street was an old mansion with a massive garden, paved in white stones. No one lived there and it had been empty for years. So, when I couldn't stand to be at home, I'd go wander in the gardens and daydream about living there. One day, a very handsome and mysterious stranger found me in my daydreams. He told me he was buying the house, and would be staying there intermittently, but that I was still welcome to wander the gardens. He was lovely and gentle, so unlike my father. We developed a friendship over time, and sometimes he'd bring me little gifts from his travels. There were murmurs about him in town and speculations of his wealth and bloodline. But I knew what he was. An elite vampire, far stronger than any turned. Than any man. But he was kind to me, and I wasn't afraid."

"One day, my father caught me leaving. He called me a vampire whore and accused me of fucking and feeding Jamison. I told him that wasn't true, that it wasn't anything like that. He didn't care. And he beat me. He beat me badly. He broke some ribs and mangled my face so much that I could barely see. I left and I ran, and I went to the only place I felt safe: the garden."

"Jamison found me there. 'What did he do to you, my pet?' he asked horrified, and when I told him, he demanded that I stay with him. He said I was special to him, and he wanted me to be safe, and that my father was too much of a coward to come to his door and demand me back. I was sixteen and in love, and so I said yes."

"That was the start of my daydream brought to life. Pretty dresses and pretty things. Jamison doted on me and gave me anything I asked for. It seemed like a paradise. Until it wasn't. When he wouldn't let me go anywhere. When he'd leave without saying goodbye or telling me where he was going. When he'd return and be disappointed I wasn't awake or present to greet him at the door. He started finding fault with everything I did. Nothing was ever good enough. 'Don't you love me, my pet?' he would say. And I'd cry and beg for forgiveness."

"One night he came home, but not alone. He had a beautiful lady on his arm, another elite. And he brought her to me, introduced me as 'his lovely pet, Violetta.' I was so confused by what was happening as he dismissed me with a wave of his hand. He kissed her there, in front of me and then he took her to bed. I felt so betrayed, I cried and cried and wouldn't leave my room for days. It hurt so badly. I think there really isn't pain quite like a broken heart."

"Finally, he came to see me. He was irritated by my upsetting behavior, and when I told him how he betrayed me, he looked at me and told me there could be no betrayal because we weren't a couple. I was, quite literally, his pet. I was not his equal and he did not share his bed with those beneath him."

"I can't believe he said that to you," Emile whispered, horror spreading across his face.

"So, I asked him to turn me."

"You . . . asked for him to turn you? Didn't you know how your life could end up?"

"I did. I didn't care. I loved him and I wanted to be with him forever. I would have done anything. So, he turned me, and he left me alone burning in fevers for days while I changed. I called for him so many times, but he never came. Eventually the fevers stopped, the morning arrived, and I awoke as something new. And I went to him and told him, now we could be together. We could start a new life; we could be happy. We could even get married. And do you know what he said to me?"

"What did he say?" Emile asked softly.

"He stroked my cheek and looked into my hope-filled face and said, 'Oh my sweet thing, how could anyone love you? Look at where you came from. You're damaged goods. But have no fear, I have just made you ten times better. Be a good girl and leave me in peace, my pet.'"

"I was already quite broken before the change," she continued. "So when I turned, I became a little more broken. All that pent-up hurt and anguish changed into something new. Into something strong. Something different. Something full of spite and hatred and *vengeance.* I looked up into that beautiful face that I loved so much. A face that I once thought was my savior. And I continued to watch that face as I drove a silver knife straight through his evil heart. And then again. And again. And again. He fell, screaming and gurgling, and I walked away. And I did not come as he called my name in his final moments."

"I left the house; I left the gardens. The pretty dresses and the dreams. And whoever the girl was that entered was not who left. I ran and I created havoc and I killed, and I loved it. Humans feared me, other turned feared me. Leaders from turned communities tried to trap me and break me, use me for their own purposes. They called me a monster— so I became one. Just not one they could leash."

"And then Annora found me, blood covered and soaked from the night rains. And she was the first being who wasn't afraid of me, who didn't try to control me, who didn't condemn me. She fed me and asked me what I wanted. 'To kill things,' I told her. 'I want to be feared so that no one can ever hurt me again.'"

"'Do you want to protect innocents while you do it?' she asked me. And I thought briefly back to the girl with the dreams and how no one had come for her. How no one had tried to save her. 'Yes,' I told her. 'Good,' was all she replied. She introduced me to this life."

"I'm so sorry about everything you've been through—"

"Don't," Violetta interrupted, holding up her hand. "I don't want your apologies. They're worthless to me. You did not do those things. Why would you apologize?"

Emile paused. "It just seems like the thing to do," he answered.

"The thing to do," she countered, "is let the past be what it is and to let it go. The past doesn't matter anymore. It is dead to me."

"It made you who you are," Emile said. "All those things . . . they made you stronger."

"No, they did not, Emile," Violetta replied. "*I* made me stronger. *I did*. Trauma doesn't make you special. People say it does because they like to hear the gritty details, the odds stacked against survival, the pain, the pleasure. But it's a lie. What makes you special is how you live after it's all over. What you do with your life after the trauma, and how you choose to survive and respond. *That's* what makes you special, and *that's* who you really are."

The two rounded another corner, returning to their original spot. The sun was just beginning to peek in the distance, soft pinks and oranges tinting the horizon, ready to light up the sky. The night was over. The day had come.

"If you're wondering who you are," Violetta said, watching the painted sky with Emile. "I suggest you stop spending so much time in the past and examine the choices you are making in the present."

Chapter Four

"Descend, oh silent mercifulness
Surrender us unto a sanctioned ground..."

Link To a New World

Emile sucked in his breath as he crossed the line into the human city. He didn't like coming to places like this, and he still didn't understand why Foxxe had felt the need to send him. He grumbled internally and thought wistfully of Ash and his rogue hunting. However, he couldn't deny the beauty he was surrounded by.

City Salvatore was a stark contrast to the town Emile and his troop lived in. The streets were busy and full of life. The buildings were attractive and well maintained. And unlike the hauntingly empty and rusted playgrounds spotting the vampire territory, children laughed and squealed on shiny swings and bright-colored slides. Or they did until Emile walked by.

For the most part, vampires didn't look all that different from humans. No extra arms like a blight, no tail like a wolfhound, not even horns like the warlocks. True, they had paler skin, pointy teeth, and slightly pointed ears, but all those things could easily be hidden. And in the beginning, Emile had tried to hide them. But something about the vampire was off-putting to humans no matter how many layers they wore, and Emile found people gave him a wide berth anywhere he went.

"They will always know," Annora had told him once. "Primal fear is a powerful thing."

Emile continued his route through the city, avoiding eye contact and moving as fast as he could without looking too suspicious. He had been tasked with the delicate job of negotiating a new blood bank that would be stationed outside of City Salvatore. There was already a human garrison stationed there, as most cities had, and with the Vampiric Legionnaires funding the blood bank building, it was an easy addition for the city that could bring them revenue and strengthen connections with vampire communities. Emile just wanted to get this over with as fast as possible. Meet with the director, explain the positives, establish a connection, get the hell out.

He was lost in his thoughts as he turned a corner, where a group of human men stood in a circle. They were smoking and laughing, no doubt relaxing after a hard day of work as Emile took in their oil stained clothes and dirt crusted skin. They zeroed in on him immediately and Emile felt the energy tense around him. As he walked by, they looked at him suspiciously, muttering under their breath.

"Filthy vamp," spat one.

Emile bristled but kept moving. He didn't want to make a scene.

"Hey!" the man called. "I said you're a filthy fucking vamp."

Emile paused, his back to the human.

"That's right," the man said. "You know what you are."

Emile blew out his breath slowly and resumed walking forward.

"Coward."

Within an exhale, Emile whipped around and stood face-to-face with his harasser. The other men took a step back as Emile threw open his coat and stood silently, his hands poised behind his back. He said nothing and just…waited.

The man gazed into Emile's crystal eyes, fear clouding his own pupils. Emile could hear the increased thudding of the man's heart, the scent of panic exuding from weather beaten skin. If he cared to look, he knew he'd see the rising hairs on his skin followed by a flood of goosebumps and cold sweat.

"Please," he gasped, almost prayer like.

"I see," Emile replied, disgusted but not breaking his eye contact. "Now who is the coward?"

Emile stepped back and returned walking toward his destination. The scent of their fear, anger, and shame lingered painfully in the air, and while some may have reveled in the bittersweet aroma, it only made Emile's rage simmer beneath his skin more than it already was.

He hated that these moments still existed. Street fights and spiteful comments. It was just one of the nails in the coffin that drove vampires and humans to create separate colonies. There were a few places, such as Gardovia, where vamps and humans lived in peace, but it was not the mainstream approach to vampiric existence. Gardovia was an idyllic dream. This was just hell.

Emile continued briskly, eager to be out of this hellhole. He wasn't used to being on his own as it was. He and Ash were together pretty much all the time, and if it wasn't Ash, it was one of the other members of Squall. He slowed his pace a bit and took back in the surroundings. Despite missing his companions, he also felt surprisingly free. Reluctant though he was to meet with the director, he had to admit it was nice to be a little independent. Even if there were some douchebags along the way.

He strode up the steps of the capitol building and handed his envelope to a patrolman standing outside the entrance. It had a large domed roof with ivory pillars running along the length of the building. It was impressive.

"I have an appointment with the director."

The guard pulled out the paper and briefly glanced down. "This says Vaughn Foxxe. You're not Vaughn Foxxe."

"No," Emile replied, pulling a sealed envelope from his vest pocket. "But I do represent him."

The guard took the sealed envelope and opened it. After careful consideration, he begrudgingly allowed Emile entrance. "Straight forward. The director insisted on greeting you in the hall."

How thoughtful, Emile thought grimly. *Probably because he doesn't trust filthy vamps.*

Emile didn't know much about this town's director. All Emile knew was that the director was relatively new and had sparked conversation and inquiries after some of his introductory legislation. Foxxe had been watching him for a while and felt he would be a good ally, but Emile didn't trust leaders and authority—there was almost always an ulterior motive.

Up the stairs and through the doors, Emile entered the domed middle room of the city's main hall. He was surprised to lay eyes on a young, attractive-looking man directing his aids.

"Sylvia Strothman needs an updated blueprint of the local cemetery and crematorium. Please make sure she gets one by Friday at the latest. Oh, and if you could please reach out to the road crews and inquire as to when they'll be finished on the north side, that would be exceedingly helpful."

One of the aids gestured in Emile's direction, and the director turned to meet Emile's gaze. His green eyes were welcoming and friendly, catching Emile off guard.

"Hello!" he greeted, extending his hand. "You must be here for Vaughn Foxxe! It's such a pleasure to meet you! I'm Lincoln Silverstone. You can call me Link if you like. Can I shake your hand?"

Emile was taken aback by the enthusiastic welcome and stuck his hand out awkwardly. "I'm Emile Thorne. Foxxe sends his regrets. It's a pleasure to meet you . . . Link."

Link shook Emile's hand firmly and without hesitation. "Likewise! I was very excited when Foxxe reached out to me about establishing a viable blood bank and resource center here in town. I think it's a fantastic opportunity."

"Yes," Emile replied suspiciously. "There are some benefits to it for all involved."

"You sound like you're not sure if you want our blood." Link cocked his neck to one side. "Have a taste if you like, I promise it's good."

Emile stopped and stood, shocked, for a moment, unsure how to respond. "Um, I'm not in the habit of drinking from the source. From the human. Person. Uh . . ."

"I'm kidding," Link replied, putting his hands up in the air and shaking them. "I obviously don't know if my blood is any good." He winked.

Emile laughed and awkwardly finger gunned. "You had me there for a second."

"Thought I'd lighten the mood a bit." Link shrugged. "Nice teeth though."

Emile blushed as much as a vampire could and suddenly felt at ease. Link was different from most of the other humans he'd been around in the last ten years. He felt . . . lighter. He smiled at Emile, flashing very human white teeth, and Emile felt an odd sense of comfort. The sensation was unsettling while simultaneously welcoming.

"Let's continue," Link said, running a hand through his dusky brown hair. It fell to his shoulders and the waves framed his face, giving him a roguish, almost wolflike, look. "This town has been cut off from the world for far too long. It's time we change that, and a blood bank is an excellent way to begin creating change."

"From what I've heard about you, you seem to have no problem creating change. Or waves."

"Ah, so my name precedes me." Link chuckled. "I admit, I am on the progressive end of things, but I was elected, so I have faith that the majority of our citizens are on the same page."

"I met a few on the way in," Emile commented. "They were less than welcoming."

Link frowned and ran his hands through his hair again. "I'm very sorry for that. There are always a few that are stuck in the past. Stuck in fear and perpetuated stereotypes."

"So . . . you believe vampires are stereotyped?"

"I do. I think humans are too, to be fair. So are wolfhounds, witches, any other being that may exist. Stereotypes exist for a reason, there's no doubt. However, many of those reasons are out-of-date or based in the tales told by those who lived before and through the war. We're not in a war anymore, why are we still living like we are?"

Link gestured for Emile and they began to walk through the capitol. The domed roof rose up around them, the walls decorated in paintings of previous leaders. "From what I know of our histories, there was bloodshed on both sides and considerable life lost in the name of power. I don't want my people to repeat that. In fact, I don't want anyone to repeat that."

"You talk as though you are well versed in vampire history and culture," Emile said. "And you speak so positively. That's a bit—"

"Odd?" Link interrupted. "Yeah, well, I don't claim to be an expert. I do think it's important to learn though and look outside my own narrow view of life. My perspective is just one of many. And I can't make the world a better place without taking into consideration the life and wellbeing of people outside of my perspective. Which is why," he concluded, "I would like to create a resource stop here for the vampire community."

"Do you worry about the backlash from the citizens who won't like what you're doing?" Emile asked.

"Of course. But my job is to look after my citizens and establish connections for a better future, regardless of the current personal or societal norms."

"So we are connections?"

"Of course you are. Everyone is! Granted some are just not as good as others. And of course everyone has a motive in their actions. But in the current political climate, where everything is a bit uneasy, I want my citizens to be protected in the event anything . . . goes south."

Emile thought for a moment. "Do you see it going south?"

Link paused thoughtfully before speaking. "I cannot speak for the political world as a whole, but yes, I can see things going awry depending on who is in charge. And I don't have great faith in those right now. They are far too consumed with power and are willing to do terrible things to get what they want. Their treatment of the wolfhounds is a prime example, and I think that vampires are not too far behind that. And somehow, I do not think that your people will go willingly."

Emile shook his head. "So you want our protection? In exchange for . . . ?"

"In exchange for our support. And for whatever voice I have in this world, in this town, in this climate. I will do everything I can to make the world a better place for everyone."

"And you have no aspirations of power?" Emile asked curiously.

"Of course I do," Link replied easily. "Anyone who tells you otherwise is lying. But I do aspire to use my status and influence well and enrich the lives of those around me. And if I ever become corrupt, you have my express permission to drain me dry." Link winked.

Emile felt a weird little tickle in his chest, and he awkwardly laughed as he frantically wondered at Link's personable behavior. He didn't know how to respond and struggled to find words, any words at all. Luckily for him, Link continued talking, unfazed and seemingly unaware of Emile's awkward desperation.

"We walked all around this building, and I was supposed to point out who was in the paintings and when it was built, but I honestly could not be more bored with that idea than I already am. Unless you want to walk around again?" Link chuckled.

Emile was puzzled to find that he did indeed want to walk through the capitol one more time with Link. Maybe two. In fact, he'd tour the whole city with Link to keep the conversation going.

Instead, he smiled and replied, "Next time for sure. Here are the plans Foxxe drew up for the blood bank and resource center and some places outside the town for a small vampire community." He drew a packet out of his vest.

"Do you think they would want to live in the town?" Link asked as he took the papers.

"I . . . don't think so," Emile replied, recalling the angry men from earlier. "But outside the city is a start. It's an adjustment for everyone involved."

"That's fair. I suppose it all takes time. Sometimes my enthusiasm gets the best of me. It was a pleasure to meet you, Emile. I hope I get to see you again sometime."

For the first time in a very long time, Emile agreed. Here was a human he wanted to see again. He couldn't explain it as he said his goodbyes and walked down the steps, his feet taking him away from Link and his growing city. Something about Link was different, and Emile had a compelling feeling that Link was somehow important and necessary. And even stranger, Emile felt a bit sad as the city faded behind him and he headed back to his home.

Chapter Five

"Cloud not our vision that we may be enlightened
To eternal life most beautiful; redemption..."

Caged Beasts Wait to Feast

It was late morning and Emile sat at the counter warming his morning Nutrimentum while idly watching old cartoons on the blinking receiver. Broadcasts hadn't quite recovered from the war. They were sketchy at best, and only certain places picked up the frequencies. He sighed as the screen flickered to black-and-white and dragged himself over to smack the receiver a couple times. *Thunk! Thunk!* The screen flashed and fixed itself, and Emile walked back behind the counter, leaning across it. He popped the tab on his drink and grimaced after his first gulp. He never did take to the taste. Distracted by the television, he took another sip.

Ash often teased him over his preference for animated shows, but for Emile they were a bit of an escape from everyday life. A little bit of his past life that was left untainted. Some bumping and thumping from the upstairs alerted him to Ash finally awakening. Emile glanced at the clock. Eleven in the morning. Well, not noon so that was something. Ash clunked down the stairs, his black hair an unruly mess around his face. Emile could not help but both admire and despise how manly and perfect Ash looked, even sleep hazed and disoriented.

"Well good morning, beauty queen." Emile teased, sliding Ash some nutrition. "Have a good night?"

Ash sucked down his breakfast and took a huge breath. "I was out late tracking some rogue vamps who have been breaking and entering at some of the blood banks." He tousled his hair and glanced at the TV. "Couldn't sleep so I decided to burn off some energy."

"Right," Emile replied. "Well you look fine. How do the rogues look?"

Ash smiled devilishly. "Rogue. Sadly only one made it back."

Emile looked at Ash suspiciously. "Only one? On purpose?"

"No, but if anybody is going to come out alive, it's going to be me. Can't solve every problem with some witty banter and a pretty smile."

Emile raised his hands defensively. "I'm just checking. We both know you've got a lust for fighting."

Ash rolled his eyes as he shoved on his boots. "Get in a couple of brawls and everyone thinks you're a bloodthirsty fighter."

"Brawls you started," Emile pointed out.

"Brawls I started because someone was being an asshole," Ash replied. "It's not my fault he was being an asshole. It's his!"

Emile gave Ash a sarcastic look. "You can't make everyone shut up."

"Then why do my fists perfectly fit a running mouth? It's a match made in heaven."

Emile chuckled and decided to let it go. Everyone knew Ash had a violent streak—when provoked. He was unable to keep his mouth shut and even more incapable of walking away from a fight. Ash was good at fights. He was good at them, and he loved them. Ash was more suited to this life than Emile ever would be. Emile wasn't a coward, he was just a turned that shouldn't have been. He made the best of his situation while Ash seemed to thrive in it.

"Rogues know what's at stake when they decide to break treaties and lines. They know what's waiting for them. And I'll not let them undo the work we've done and the home we've built." Ash spoke confidently as he poured himself another drink, this once laced with some fresh blood he'd brought home.

They both sat silently as the characters raced across the screen, saving the city from certain destruction. Just when all seemed lost, there they were, the defenders of the city! Emile liked this one best, heroes that also lived in shadows and didn't belong to the human world. They had their own community, their own family.

"Which one is your favorite?" Ash asked, nodding toward the television.

"The purple one."

"I like the red one."

"Of course, you do. He's angry and hostile. Just like you!"

Ash rolled his eyes and then shrugged his shoulders. He swiftly stood and turned back to the staircase. "I'm getting dressed," he threw over his shoulder. "And then we're leaving."

Emile clicked a response and turned to the sink to wash their cups. Their home was small but comfortable, a quiet townhouse in the leftovers of a once-bustling city. Like many towns ravaged by the war, it was a vampire-only community. The laws of the vampire world were simple: leave humans alone, live your life quietly, and don't break lines between blood banks. Each vampire community had their own leaders and blood supply lines—and you didn't infringe on another community. And it wasn't that vampires were forbidden in the human world. They just didn't fit in. Vaughn Foxxe had told them of several vampires who lived and thrived in human companionship, but those cases were few and far between and often helped by wealth and influence. Emile didn't know what that was like. After he had been turned, he had run from his community.

Emile washed the blood mixture out of their cups and watched it spin down the drain, mixing with the water. Together yet apart. He closed his eyes and tried to think back to the moment of his rebirth—of his death. But he was only met with flashing images and the horrible cries of his parents and little sister. Then...nothing. Nothing until he woke up with Ash beside him. Ash had always been there. Emile closed his eyes, his fingers curling around the counter edge. He tried so hard to remember. He wanted to remember what happened that day. To him and his family. Slaughtered by vampires.

"Red. Everything was red."

But the memories were as the water and blood. Together yet apart. Ash had been away during the attack and had returned to find Emile gasping for air, changing into a turned. In the days that followed, Emile had been consumed with raging fevers and hallucinations while Ash oversaw burying the dead. When the fevers broke and Emile rose . . . he left. He left and could not bear to look back. Sometimes when all was quiet and he allowed himself to remember, he regretted never saying goodbye.

"Have you seen my new belt?" Ash asked, thundering down the stairs once more.

"Slung over the sofa, naturally," Emile replied, turning off the water and shaking his head.

"Naturally." Ash dodged into the small sitting room.

"Slob."

"Virgin."

"I'll never understand why that's an insult," Emile replied, throwing his hands in the air. "Truly, is that the best you've got?"

"Fine. Smart-mouth."

"Manwhore."

"Whoa, whoa, whoa. If I can't shame you for yours, you can't shame me for mine."

"I never said you couldn't, I just said it was dumb." Emile snickered as they walked out the door.

Ash locked it behind them, and they bounded down the steps. Emile was struck by the emptiness of the streets. He'd never noticed it before but having now been in City Salvatore, he finally noticed the stillness.

Emile looked to the other half of the townhouse. "When was the last time you think he was home?"

"Been awhile I suspect, based on the leaves in front of the door," Ash replied. "But you know Foxxe, always moving, always something going on. He's got dealings we will likely never know about. But he takes care of his people. He's certainly taken care of us."

"Yes he has. And I suppose it's not really an inconvenience that we share half his house since he's never home."

The sun was hazy in the street as they stepped out, a slight chill in the air heralding the beginnings of fall. Hooded and cloaked from head to toe, they walked fast, avoiding puddles and casually nodding to their neighbors. Elites had little to no tolerance for sunshine, but the sun was a little more forgiving to the turned.

Ash and Emile continued briskly, winding their way down streets and alleyways. They had no need of a personal car since they used the company equipment for jobs, and where they lived provided easy access to their favorite meeting place: the Sentimental Dead.

Emile paused outside, no trace of the druggies from the other night. The street was quiet. Empty.

The soft repellant of magic surrounding the building almost glistened in the autumn light. As a turned, Emile still felt it, slightly, as it ruffled his hair passing in. He was grateful for that little piece of leftover humanity. Both Ash and Emile nodded and waved respectfully to Sean, noting the few vampires languishing at the bar and front tables. Soft, brooding music wound its way in the atmosphere, as if caressing the sad souls who lingered there.

If we have souls, Emile thought bitterly. He wasn't sure they did. If he did.

Heading right and to the back where the booths lay alone and undisturbed, Ash and Emile came upon the rest of their company. Violetta was leaned against the wall, sharpening a knife from her ridiculous corset, her blond hair piled on top of her head in a messy bun. She wore a long-sleeved plum top and black leggings with knee-high army boots. Annora wore a matching outfit sans corset, opting for a thick black belt that accentuated her full form while holding lethal darts and daggers. Her long, black hair was swept out of her face on either side with silver combs, which left her curls trailing down her back. Two daggers poked out of the top of her boots. Both were outfitted for travel. Annora hunched over the table beside Foxxe surveying reports and maps.

"Good morning, boys," Foxxe greeted. "Or should I say afternoon?" Amusement twinkled in his blue eyes. His blond hair was swept to the nape of his neck in a graceful, subtle knot above the collar of his coat. A few stray hairs fell into his face, which had returned to the papers on the table. If Ash was a dark god, Foxxe would be the golden one. His dress and manners harkened back to the age of gentlemanly grace and splendor, a slight accent in his voice that betrayed his presence among natives. He was a general, a commander, a war hero and yet, still soft, as though the world had tried to break him but couldn't. "I see we have one rogue in detention."

"Ah yes, the others weren't nearly as agreeable," Ash replied.

"Well I'm glad you at least brought one back," Foxxe answered. "The rogues are getting out of hand, and nobody wants to take responsibility for them. None of the surrounding vampire councils claim to have any part in their escapades. We have to get them under control, people are disappearing and dying thanks to this infestation. We have to find out who is leading their rebellion. There's always a leader.

"On top of that, there's been more reports of blights in these surrounding areas." Foxxe pointed to the map. "We're going to split up, patrol the grounds, and find out if the locals have seen or smelled anything out of the ordinary. Emile, you go with Annora to pick up some supplies. Ash and Violetta, you inspect the vehicles and weapons and make sure they're ready to go. I'm going to speak to some of my patrols and make sure our territory is covered while we are gone. Meet back here ASAP. By the way, Emile, Lincoln had wonderful things to say about you. He said you played your ambassador role very well." Foxxe smiled.

Emile flushed slightly at the mention of Link's name. He'd fallen asleep last night pondering over the curious level of comfort he had found there. Mostly he found himself thinking of Link's wolfish grin and how lovely his neck looked when he had offered it to him.

"You didn't bring up how your diplomatic trip went," Ash commented suspiciously, clearly noting the slight pink on Emile's face.

"It was fine. It was good!" Emile replied. "I think Link—Lincoln—will be a great addition to our public relations."

"Interesting," Ash replied, intrigued. "You'll have to tell me all about that later. Think you can get your hands dirty changing tires, princess?" Ash joked with Violetta.

"As if. You can do it and I'll supervise." Violetta sassed.

"Because you don't know how?"

"Because I just don't want to," she replied and waltzed out the door.

For a split second Ash grinned after her, but the grin vanished as he punched Emile in the arm.

"Hey what's that for?!"

The grin returned as Ash cocked his head. "To remind you: I'll beat you if you're dumb."

"As if," Emile retorted. "I can take you any day."

Ash cocked his fingers in salute and walked backward and out the door, following Violetta. God help the two of them alone together all day. Or maybe it would be exactly what they needed. Emile was confused by their situationship. They weren't quite a couple but they also kind of were. Back and forth, back and forth they danced the dance of what if and maybe.

"Commander Hoyt will meet you and get you everything we will need. You will also drop off these." Foxxe handed a bundle of papers to Emile.

"These are copied reports of blights and rogues. I want them to stay up-to-date and aware."

"Not a problem," Annora replied. "We will be on our way then." She turned and beckoned Emile to follow.

Emile glanced at Foxxe contemplating a conversation about Link and City Salvatore. But Foxxe was absorbed in other inquiries, and Emile decided not to disturb him. Plus, he knew better than to keep Annora waiting. That was something you just didn't do.

Annora commanded her space without even trying. If she spoke, you listened. Perhaps that was part of her unique gifts, the power of influence. All elites came with special abilities. Call it magic, evolutionary development, maybe a solid blend of both. Annora could sway those in her presence just by her facial expressions and commanding voice. It was a lethal force in battle with other turned vampires or humans—not so much with blights. But Annora was an old elite with plenty of time to practice her gifts, and Emile made sure to show proper respect. Though he knew she didn't use those gifts on her companions—that was a level of trust that could not be broken.

He had never spent too much one-on-one time with Annora. Most of the time she merely observed rather than engaged. Any missions she went on were either solo or with Violetta, and any patrols they shared were typically silent affairs. Emile knew little about Annora's past—other than that she had been birthed in an elite facility and had been trained as a weapon for them before becoming disillusioned with elite rhetoric. Emile both respected and feared her. He remembered the first time he met her. He had been bragging about his recent rogue takedown and Foxxe asked him to show his skills—against Annora. Needless to say, she handed his ass to him in a matter of minutes. Emile was almost certain that she was a goddess. Annora was both beautiful and destructive. Sometimes he felt that strange little urge to flirt, but he kept that to himself most of the time. He supposed most beings felt that way around Annora though. How could you not?

The ride to the blood bank and supply depot was uneventful, but incredibly comfortable, Emile noted, as they rode smoothly in the vehicle Foxxe had given them.

"We're all going to die someday," Foxxe had said. "Might as well be comfortable on the ride." Foxxe had worked with machinists and designers to create special vehicles for vamps. They mimicked vehicles from before the war but were designed to traverse all environments and worked on alternative fuels and steam systems. They were fast, quiet, and armored. Perfect for hunting blights and rogues.

As they rode up to the gate, Annora leaned out and keyed in their password. The gate opened up to another stop where Annora scanned her personnelle key card.

"How many?" asked a voice from the box. It came off grainy and ended with static interference.

"Two," Annora replied. Emile leaned forward and waved to the camera.

"What's up, Commander?!"

Annora leaned back as the gate raised and they rode in, pulling up to the command center. Around them, soldiers marched in formation, practicing drills and moving supplies. On each arm at the shoulder was the patch of alliance—a skull with vampire fangs surrounded by angel wings. Emile found it both amusing and distasteful, comparing vampires and angels. But these men wore it proudly. Or at least most of them did. Some of the civilians in the compound eyed them warily and pulled back behind the soldiers. As if Emile and Annora were monsters. As if *they* were dinner.

"Commander Hoyt!" Annora greeted, extending her hand. "Thank you for helping us out on such short notice."

"It's not a problem," he replied, shaking her hand firmly and without hesitation. "We are more than happy to assist in any way."

Emile stepped forward. "It's been a while since I've seen you, Commander, how have you been surviving without me?"

He smiled warmly and embraced Emile. "It's good to see you, son."

The shock of the hug was nothing new as Emile returned the embrace, before stepping back and handing him the papers. "Foxxe sent these for you."

Annora filled him in as the commander surveyed the details on the papers. Emile observed the man, his hair a little more silver than the last time. Both Emile and Ash had spent time in the military prior to Foxxe, earning their keep by patrolling stations, raiding rogue vampires, and assisting in blight tracking. The commander had been younger then but still fatherly toward the two vamps. He had pushed them and trained them and made Emile feel like he had purpose, like he had a reason to keep going. But relationships between humans and vampires were tenuous, even in arms, and the government began treating enlisted vampires as weapons or tools rather than soldiers or people with needs and rights. Ash and Emile had quietly left after their term was up. They had wandered for a few days before Foxxe caught up to them and offered a new path. Emile much preferred his new life in Squall, but he was grateful for the kindness that the Commander had always shown Ash and Emile. It was not something he would forget. Ever.

The commander rubbed his forehead, looking very tired. "Tell Foxxe thank you. It's hard to keep tabs on these things. There's been an uptick in missing people, break-ins and thievery. It's been hard to keep up with since our funding has diminished."

It was no secret that the government had cut funding to the Vampire Legionnaires. Communication between elites and human leaders had broken down. People were scared of the random blight outbursts, of the rogues, of vampires in general. Politicians looked better severing ties with vampiric aid—after all, how can you trust a monster?

"People are missing?" Emile asked, frowning.

"People are always missing, but there seems to be more lately. No discernible patterns—old, young, doesn't matter."

"Do you have people looking for them?"

"We do the best we can with what we have. But you know the statistics on the likelihood of them coming home."

"Foxxe will be happy to add it to the patrols, if you have a list or descriptions," Annora said.

"That would be very helpful. I appreciate any insight Foxxe might have." Commander Hoyt gestured to a worker to print out the details.

"As you know, we're leaving to patrol some of the surrounding areas. Have you gotten any word on rogue leaders around here?" Annora asked.

"Sadly no. They're here. Then they're not. They don't linger long enough for us to catch them and ask questions."

"Ash brought one in the other day," Emile interjected. "I'm sure we can get something from him."

"I heard about that," Commander Hoyt replied. "I see Ash hasn't changed much. Four rogues and only one comes home."

"Wouldn't want to change him," Annora said. "You need that kind of attitude in this line of work."

"I don't begrudge the boy his fire, he's certainly earned his steel," Hoyt replied. "He's a better fit there than he ever was here." He chuckled.

As they were wrapping up, a car rolled beside the curb outside the building. It was long and sleek, painted a shiny black. If Emile could have turned colder, he would have as he watched the doors open and Admiral Rawlings stepped out. Rawlings was a tall, thin, sallow man who simultaneously denied a vampire's right to exist while still demanding loyalty and credence. Emile hated him. Rawlings was an active force in slashing the Vampiric Legionnaires' budget and was a social figure who openly perpetuated hate and bigotry.

He walked up the steps followed by foot soldiers, ready and waiting for his command.

"I was not aware," the admiral droned, "that we'd be entertaining . . . *them* . . . today." The disdain in his voice was hard and sharp and he side-eyed Emile and Annora as if they were an unexpected pest.

"It was an impromptu arrangement," Commander Hoyt explained. "Vaughn Foxxe's company is currently hunting blights and requested supplies for an extended departure. We also were not aware you would be coming today."

"I am not obligated to tell you anything. And where exactly are these blights? I have not received any intelligence on the matter," Rawlings asked, sounding slightly bored.

Annora stepped aside as Hoyt showed the admiral the latest reports. Emile hung back, rage seething under his skin. Rawlings stood silently as the commander spoke, shrouded in his black coat. Looking like death personified.

"Hmmm. Well, I guess it takes one to track one," the admiral replied. "Nothing can replace pure animal instinct. Tell me, *boy*"—he sneered at Emile—"how does it feel hunting what you will one day become? Do you see yourself in their faces?"

Emile seethed inside and replied, "I don't know, do you see your face when you slaughter human men in the name of war and salvation?"

"Anyone who is a threat to my country is no better than rabid, feral creatures. Including ones in the making. Or," he said glancing at Annora, "ones that ought to be caged."

Emile took a step forward but Annora held up her hand. "A caged beast is far more dangerous than a free one," she replied, unfazed. "They've nothing to do but sit. And wait. Come Emile. His stench is aggravating my inner beast."

Without another word, Annora turned from the raging admiral and walked out the door. Emile followed suit. They had won this battle, but Emile did not feel like a victor. With people such as the Admiral in charge and commanding not just an army but a nation, the hope for a better future remained dim. People like him thrived on division and chaos, holding power over marginalized beings and perpetuating stereotypes and outdated narratives. After all, a nation divided is much easier to control.

"I don't understand why they hate us so much," Emile said, exasperated. A look over his shoulder and the admiral's footmen were at attention, watching their every move. There was no admiration or respect in their watchful eyes. Only fear and disgust.

"Why wouldn't they?" asked Annora as she loaded their supplies.

"Because we're helping them. This is a business transaction! Plus we've never harmed them. We protect them!"

"True. But that doesn't undo the years before us and the legends that forever branded us as monsters."

"But *we* didn't do that—we're different! We're changing the narrative; we're making their lives better!" Emile looked at her with desperation. "Doesn't that count? Doesn't that count for *something*?"

Annora paused and studied his face. "Oh, Emile. You've heard the stories of our ancestors. Pale, handsome creatures that lingered in dark places terrified of the sun? Mortal humans made us into monsters for fear of their own dark hearts."

"We may have been monsters back then but we aren't now."

Annora looked at him sadly. "Fear has a way of changing the past sometimes.Twisting it. Reforming it into something more...palatable for specific groups of people. The stories of vampires as bloodthirsty savages may be true, but have you ever wondered why this fear and hatred runs so deeply? Where it all began?" Annora paused and surveyed the flow of life around her. "When vampires came into this world, we were not welcomed. We were not loved. We were not wrapped in soft blankets and handed to glowing mothers. We were seen as abominations, as sins. We could not be understood, and so humans do what they do best when they are afraid—they destroy."

Emile paused as the realization set in. "Mortal humans made us into monsters for fear of their own dark hearts . . ."

Annora held his gaze ". . . the poison of humanity ebbing in their veins. Their own dark presence haunted by the sun for the evil things they did out of fear. And fear is a powerful emotion. What followed was an unholy devastation masked by religion and self-righteous virtues. Vampire babes and their mothers slaughtered mercilessly and without reproach. Some vampire children were stolen and sent to camps where they were experimented on and underwent horrible treatments to try and change them. Make them human. Make them palatable. We think of humans as an intellectual species for what do humans crave above all else? Understanding. When that is unattainable, they are engulfed by fear. And when fear is in control, millions will suffer. We didn't have to be monsters." Annora breathed. "But we had to fight to survive. We met blood with blood and carved out our spot in the world that desperately wished us gone. And while pain should not be returned for pain, and only darkness can come from cyclical trauma, sometimes you have to be what they say you are to make it out alive. Doesn't make it any better.

But at least you're alive. And if you're lucky, you'll find yourself with other survivors who are ready to break the cycle."

"Survivors like Squall," Emile said.

Annora nodded her head. "Yes, survivors like Squall and like so many other companies that do what we do. We can't change the past. Sometimes we cannot change the present. But the future holds limitless potential, and I like to think the stories we create now will eventually overshadow and replace the ones from the past."

Annora closed the hatch and climbed into the driver's seat. Emile followed to the passenger side, feeling pensive. He hadn't really known about the firstborn vampires and the savagery of their demise. He'd never cared to know.

The ride back was quiet, and Emile realized he didn't know much about the history of vampires—or at least, he only knew what he had been taught. What he read and what he watched. But did he want to know more? Emile had always been content hating his existence and resenting his new life. It had only been worthwhile because of Ash. Ash and then the rest of his company. They had become like a second family and Emile realized, for the first time, that he had never considered them monsters. The rule had never held for Foxxe, Violetta, or Annora.

So why did the rule hold for him?

Chapter Six

"Our precious evolutions undone and abolished
Bless us oh wheel of fortune..."

Ash might track the rogues and bring them in, but Foxxe was the one who took over when they returned to the jailhouse. Built underground, beneath the local vampire chapter, it was the perfect place to hold rogue vampires as it was soundproof and not easily accessible to unauthorized beings. Emile had asked once why they didn't just take rogues straight to the compound and Commander Hoyt. Foxxe had replied that, although they worked together, they were still separate, and the interrogation and sentencing were left to the vampire company in the area they were captured. Much like when human rogues were caught by vampires and turned over to the proper authorities, everyone kept to their own kind.

"It takes a vampire to question a vampire," Foxxe had told him once. "And sometimes the techniques are less than savory."

Today Emile joined Foxxe at the Sentimental Dead before heading out to their official headquarters. Foxxe liked meeting at the Sentimental Dead prior and after to discuss details. He didn't trust all of the vampires stationed at headquarters. Some of them were too closely tied to elites for Foxxe's comfort. All it took was one wrong word and elites would be breathing down Foxxe's back, and it didn't take much since most of the elites regarded both Foxxe and Annora as traitors. Emile had asked Foxxe once what kept the elites from taking them out once and for all.

"Connections. Some good, some I wish didn't exist. Life is all about connections and who you know and what you can do for those people you know."

Today Foxxe seemed a bit distracted as they hurried on their way, the sun sinking into the distant landscape of shrubby trees. Emile appreciated that he wasn't living in a heavily populated vamp city. Since he had grown up on a farm, it was comforting to be in a quiet place—even though the old town sometimes invited unsavory folks.

Like drugged vampires, Emile thought ruefully, recalling the events he had witnessed a few days ago. Vampires passing through, holing up in abandoned buildings. It was true that blood prostitution wasn't *illegal*. It was more along the lines of "keep it in your city and don't bring it to mine." It was too hard a system to control, so the best they could do was attempt to contain it to one area. But sometimes it leaked out. Emile hated them. He hated them because of what that life had cost Ash. He'd seen the damage firsthand, and he was not a fan.

They rounded the corner and came up to a walled-off building. The wall itself stood eighteen feet high, topped with metal spikes and merged together in a twisted wrought iron gate. Foxxe pushed the gate open and both he and Emile climbed the wide steps leading into the building. Ironically, it was an old brick church, partially destroyed from the war. Foxxe had bought the property for the vampire headquarters after settling in the town and had it remodeled with the addition of the wall outside. In case of an attack or natural disaster, it was meant to act as a safehouse as well as a headquarters. Pushing open the heavy wooden double doors, Foxxe greeted the vamps lingering inside.

It may have been a church once, but the inside held no pews or choir chambers. Instead, desks littered with papers and empty cups, bookshelves filled haphazardly, and tired-looking hunters and word keepers filled the massive building. Emile knew there were levels above them but had never been. Ash had been there once and said it was mostly sleeping areas for hunters and companies traveling between stations. In the far back was a gymnasium where vamps could practice and train and an old kitchen fully stocked with Nutrimentum and emergency blood.

"Stylos!" Foxxe greeted heartily. "Haven't seen you in quite a while!" He shook hands with a massively muscled vampire. Emile swallowed as he took the giant in. Stylos stood well over six feet, with impressive arms and legs rippled in finely developed muscles. He was completely bald save for a red mustache that elegantly peaked at the tips.

"It is good to see you too, Foxxe," he replied enthusiastically. "You must be Emile. We've never met but I've heard about you." He extended a hand to Emile.

Emile took it and shook and breathed a sigh of relief when his hand wasn't crushed in the giant's grasp. "I've heard of you as well, sir. One of Foxxe's top commanders in the war! Led one of the most successful underground campaigns during a hostage situation and saved countless beings' lives."

"I see you know our history," Stylos replied, clearly pleased.

"And now Stylos hunts blights and rogues on the side with his own company, Tempest," said Foxxe.

"I'm glad we caught you. How long will you be in town?"

"My company has already passed through; I was just tying up some loose ends," Stylos replied.

"Have time for a drink with your old war pal before you go?"

"Foxxe, you know I always have time to drink!" Stylos replied, crooking his arm around Foxxe's neck and laughing.

Foxxe patted Stylos on the back. "Wonderful! Emile and I have an interrogation to do first. Why don't you head over to the Sentimental Dead after you're done, and we'll meet you there. Tell the barkeep to put it on my tab."

"I was going to do that anyway," Stylos replied, lumbering to the stairs. "See you soon, boys! Bring your drinking game with you when you come!"

Stylos began climbing up, the steps thundering and creaking as he went. Emile was sure he'd never met anyone like Stylos before and was relieved he was on Foxxe's side.

He followed Foxxe down the stairs to a dimly lit hallway. While the world upstairs was cluttered with wooden desks, old books, and soft light, down below it was much more primitive. Holding cells were carved out of the dirt and covered in stone. Emile felt the air get a bit colder and damper as he descended. Finally, Foxxe made a turn to the left, into a hallway with rows of cells. At the end was a desk occupied by a young-looking vampire, his legs sprawled across the top, casually watching old television shows on a banged-up receiver.

"I'd like prisoner A46 brought to the detention room, please," Foxxe said.

"Soon as this is done." The vamp didn't look up.

Foxxe planted his fists into the desk and leaned across before quietly whispering, "I said, I'd like prisoner A46 brought to the detention room. Please."

The vampire looked up at Foxxe's frowning face and jumped to attention.

"Commander Foxxe, I'm so sorry. I didn't realize it was you."

"What's your name?"

"F-Frederick."

"Well, Frederick, if you're told to do your job, it doesn't matter who asked you," Foxxe replied. "Now do it."

"Yes, sir," the vamp answered quickly before scurrying away.

Foxxe rubbed his forehead tiredly. "These young recruits get worse and worse. Fresh bittens often end up in the vampire leagues before they're fully adjusted to their new life, and then they end up in jobs like this because they have no drive or passion and don't know what to do with their life."

"I suppose that's how Ash and I ended up in the military," Emile replied thoughtfully. "It seemed like the best place to go at the time."

"So many think so," Foxxe replied, circling the desk and opening the wide metal door behind it.

The detention room was stoned in like the rest of the jail cell. One lonely desk and some chairs sat near the doors, and in the middle of the room was a metal chair bolted into the floor. Iron loops protruded from each arm for chaining in the being. Emile was glad he had never been on that end. Foxxe sat down in one of the chairs and beckoned Emile to sit next to him. He then leaned back in his chair and lit a cigar.

This was not the first time Emile had seen Foxxe do an interrogation, but it was always a bit fascinating watching Foxxe settle into the role he was about to play. On a day-to-day basis, Foxxe was mild mannered, quiet, and a bit of a recluse. But when it came to interacting with elites or interrogating rogues, Foxxe's true inner power rang out. Annora's was to command. Foxxe's was to intimidate.

The door opened and Frederick rushed in the rogue Ash had detained. Emile could tell that Frederick was still feeling flustered as he chained the rogue into the chair at the center of the room. His hands slipped around the chains and he fumbled with the locks. Emile felt for him a little bit. It was something to meet Foxxe for the first time.

He and Ash had met Foxxe once while still employed in the military. Foxxe had been discussing his new headquarters with Commander Hoyt when Ash and Emile had been called in for a reprimand. Emile had met a handful of Elites but not one like Foxxe. He had read of this gallant war hero but had never expected to meet him face to face. His first impression was that of awe and fear. Foxxe was stern, certain of his actions and speech. Emile could tell he had seen death and trauma by the way he spoke. Tired. Determined. Foxxe was the first Elite that Emile had any real respect for. He was honored and relieved when Foxxe pursued him and and Ash when they left their military career.

Emile shifted his attention to the rogue. This one was tall and skinny, with unkempt dark hair and worn-out jeans. Across his pale arms Emile could see the beginnings of black veins. This vamp had been feeding on corrupted blood and probably hadn't consumed a clean source in a while. As if to confirm Emile's suspicions, the rogue leaned back in the chair, and smiled sarcastically at Foxxe and Emile, his face covered in infected lesions, his teeth rotted and brown.

"Almost feels like a party with these chains and dim lights. Where's the good blood to really get the vibes going?"

"You can go now, Frederick," Foxxe said, dismissing the anxious vampire. "I'll put him back, you can go home for the evening."

"Yes, sir, Commander Foxxe. Thank you," Frederick replied and dipped out of the room. Emile half smiled at his eagerness to depart. Definitely a newer recruit.

Foxxe sat quietly, contemplating the rogue before him and enjoying his cigar. He made no move to talk, instead leaning back with his feet up and across the desk. He was unhurried. Emile was familiar with Foxxe's tactics and also took a relaxed attitude, as if the vampire chained across from them didn't even exist. This wasn't Emile's first time. Foxxe had decided it would be good for Emile to learn this part of the job and brought him frequently to interrogations. The silence continued for several moments until the rogue finally spoke again.

"Is this what we're going to do all night?" he said. "Sit here and stare at each other? We could have done that in my cell, and I would have been much more comfortable."

Foxxe and Emile did not reply and continued to sit in silence.

"So this is what you do? You try to make me uncomfortable by not talking?" Silence.

"I know who you are," the rogue said. "You're Vaughn Foxxe. Legendary war hero and betrayer to his kind. I'm not surprised to see you here, human-loving scum."

"And I'm not surprised to see you here, Branswick, thieving vampire scum," Foxxe finally replied through the haze of cigar smoke.

The vampire looked noticeably surprised at Foxxe's words but tried to shake it off.

"That's right," Foxxe continued. "I know who you are too. I know who you are, where you live, and what you do." He smothered the butt of his cigar on the table, burning a mark into the wood. "I know who turned you and I know where your family lives. Tell me, was it hard leaving your daughter behind when you decided a life of crime was more worthwhile than that of fatherhood? She talked about you an awful lot. Sad since you just abandoned her."

Branswick's head shot up in fear, his face frozen.

"She's a darling little girl. Big brown eyes and the most adorable freckles. So friendly, too, took my hand and showed me her favorite flowers in the garden. Marigolds. So bright and lovely. Just like her. Not that you know. Or will ever know, now."

"What have you done?" Branswick gasped. "Where is my child, what did you do to her?"

Foxxe leaned forward, his elbows on his knees, his hands clasped together. He cocked his head to one side but said nothing. "Oh, you care?"

"Please," Branswick pleaded. "It was just a job. Me and my buddies were given a route of towns to disturb. We were told to be loud about it, make a big noise like a distraction."

Foxxe didn't say anything. He simply continued to stare at the vamp who was growing more desperate.

"You, listen!" Branswick squeaked to Emile. "I'm not the one who killed any of the humans, and Janelle was the one who carted off the live ones! I swear, all I did was bust up a few blood banks, I didn't know about the other stuff until it was too late!"

"I'm afraid you're guilty by association," Emile replied. "Your friends decided not to cooperate and well, now they're dead. So, that just leaves you."

"We were hired by a third party out in Moon City. I was looking for work to send money to Rosemary. I'm not . . . I'm not allowed to see her anymore, but I still try to take care of her. I didn't abandon her! This was just a good-paying job."

"You've been entrenched with the elite establishment since you were fresh bitten," Foxxe interrupted. "This wasn't a random job; you knew the stakes and so did your companions. That's why they're dead. You just had a little too much to live for. You got sloppy, Branswick. And now you've been caught."

Branswick sat silent for a moment, contemplating his next choices. Emile could tell that his daughter was important to him, but didn't think he was above using her for emotional manipulation.

"You had a choice, Branswick. When you were turned, I came to you, remember?" Foxxe said rising from his chair. "I offered you a place in my recruits. An easy life, a comfortable life. A life where you could watch your daughter grow up." Foxxe walked closer before squatting down and making eye contact with the rogue. "But I guess money and status will always win out, won't they? Easy to blend in with the crowd that has no morals rather than irritating groups like mine that force you to stay in line. I hope you're happy with your choice." A cold and calculating chill entered Foxxe's tone as he breathed out the next sentence. "Because now you'll *never* see your daughter grow up." He rose and turned on his heels as if to leave and beckoned Emile to come as well.

"You're a goddamned monster!" Branswick screamed, struggling and heaving in his chains, the metal cuffs serrating his skin that was desperately attempting to knit itself back together. "I'll kill you, Foxxe, I'll kill all of you! You murdered my daughter for the sake of your crusade?! You think you're better than the elites? You're just the same! They're swiping children off the street, too, turning them and killing them for their own goddamn war! Rosemary was innocent! She was only six!"

Foxxe stopped and listened, before he smiled and winked at Emile. He slowly turned around as though offended.

"Oh no, you misunderstand me, Branswick," Foxxe replied, sounding irritated. "No, you see, I didn't murder Rosemary. No, in fact, I saved her."

Branswick's face froze, confusion clouding his features. "You're lying. Saved her from what?"

Foxxe and Emile sat back down and Foxxe leaned back, distraught. "Well you see, Branswick, news of your failed escapade made it back to the beings who hired you. And guess what? They're not happy with you. Do you know what elites do when they're unhappy with their workers? They take out their family."

Something stirred in Emile and his mind flashed with images of his own family, brutally massacred. Bodies strewn in chaos, blood splattered and coating the furniture and floor. He closed his eyes and forced the memories away. Now was not the time.

"Rosemary and her mother were left alone and undefended when the elites sent their rogues to do what they do best: murdering innocents in the name of their crusade." Foxxe paused, allowing Branswick to panic. "But when they arrived," he continued, "they found an empty house and no trace of a freckled six-year-old girl and her mother."

"So . . . she's alive? She's okay? Where's Rosemary, where did you take her?" Branswick asked desperately.

"Both her and her mother are safe. You're concern for your ex's well-being is so . . . heartwarming."

"I got nothing against Elaine, but Rosemary is the one I care about. Why would you tell me I would never see her again? Just to work me up and get me to say what you wanted?!"

Foxxe leaned forward. "Because I'm giving you a chance to save your daughter's life."

"What are you talking about?"

"You're a scumbag, Branswick, you always have been. Even in The Before. You made piss-poor choices and now your family is paying the price."

"Thanks so much for reminding me what a shitty father I am," Branswick replied. "Consider it noted. What am I supposed to do about it now? How can you possibly guarantee my child's safety?"

"Because I'm going to put you back in your cell and I'm going to leave it unlocked. You're going to escape tonight while there's a distraction. You're going to slip out the back of this station as if you had never been jailed."

"You're . . . going to let me go?" he asked critically.

"You're going to slip out. And then you're going to die," Foxxe replied leaning back into his chair.

"What are you saying?"

"You're going to escape tonight and be killed by the guards once you're outside the gate," Emile said quietly. "There will be a huge fuss about it, that you got out before interrogation, and you'll be reported as just another drugged-up rogue who got caught and panicked when the high started wearing off. When the guard came to check on you, you knocked him out before running out of the building. Your ex got tired of you popping back into her life, so she and Rosemary relocated for her daughter's safety. It'll go back through the right channels and the beings you work for won't be so concerned about looking for your little girl once they feel comfortable knowing their vampire wasn't pressed for details."

Branswick sat quietly, his head down. Emile wondered if he would do this for his child. If he would give one last effort to keep her safe. As if in answer, Branswick raised his head, tears flowing across his weather-beaten face.

"And you *promise* me that she'll be safe?" Branswick whispered to Foxxe.

"You have my word," Foxxe replied. "Rosemary and her mother will always be under my protection, and they will always be cared for. Do this for her, so she can have a better life. Make the right choice this time," he added gently.

Branswick nodded. "I really don't know who hired us. I didn't know about all the extra stuff the other two were doing until after the fact. I only know we were hired in Moon City. We weren't the only ones either, at the turned house for hire. That's all I know."

"I know," Foxxe replied.

"If you know then why do all of this?"

"Confirmation," Foxxe answered. "And to save Rosemary."

"Why do you care about my child? You've made it clear what a terrible being I am," Branswick said.

"You're a gods-awful being," Foxxe answered. "Of that there is no denying. But your daughter isn't. She's young and innocent and full of potential. I lived through the war, I saw the destruction and death of every species, of every age. I'm tired of seeing good beings perish because the rest of us were too busy slaughtering each other. I'm tired of it. I'm tired of death."

Emile caught the sadness and desperation in Foxxe's tone, and he wondered if Foxxe's thoughts involved a beautiful woman and a lonely vampire man who used to pick her wildflowers in the middle of a war-torn world.

"Make this world a better place," Branswick replied. "Make it worthwhile."

It was in silence that Foxxe and Emile escorted Branswick back to his cell. In silence that Foxxe nodded to the vampire on duty as he and Emile walked out of the building. In silence that they departed the property and walked into the darkness. And in darkness they remained as they walked farther and farther away. Silence—until a single scream pierced the air. A scream of pain, of fear, of desperation. And then the scream faded, and they were once again left in silence.

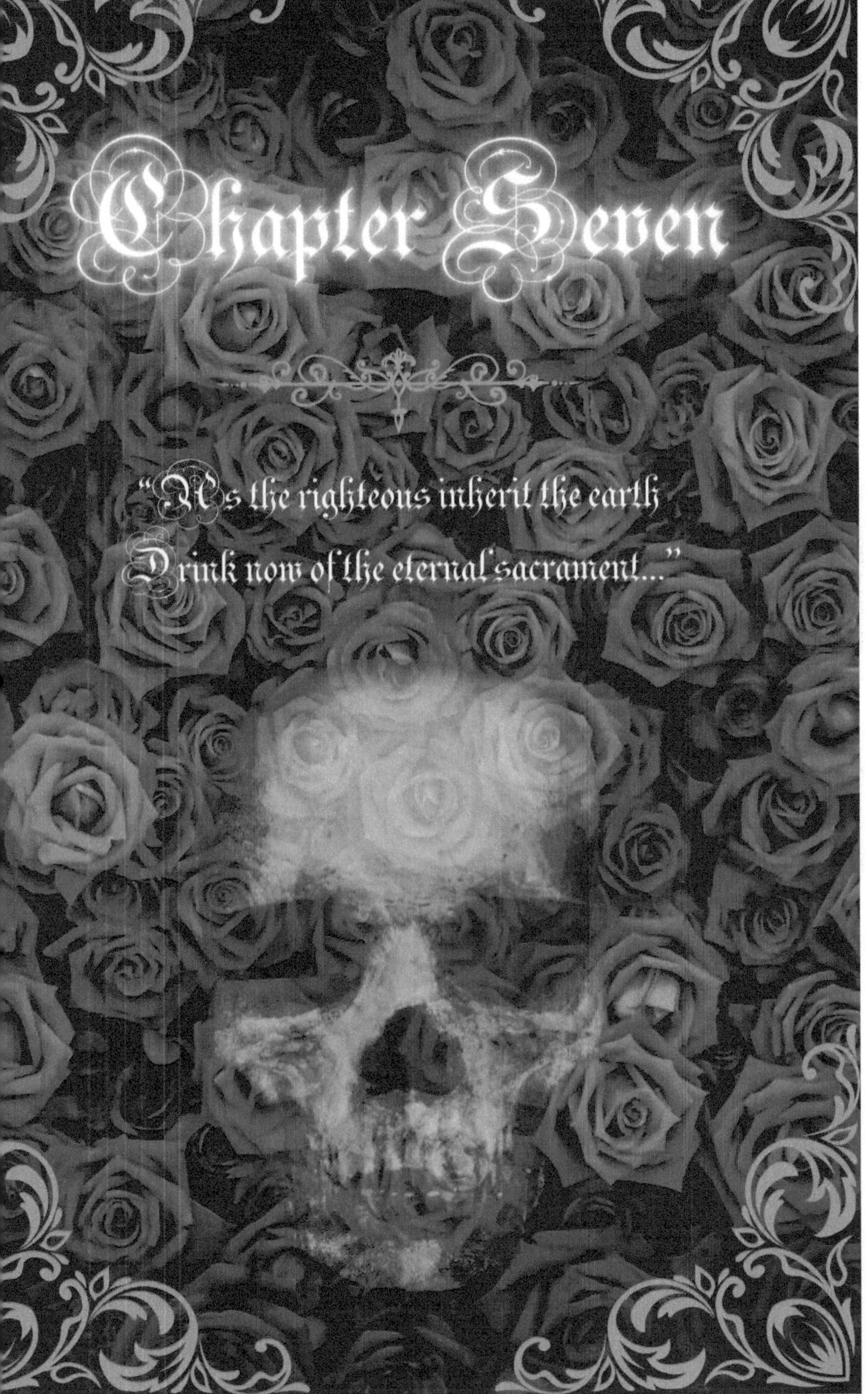

Chapter Seven

"As the righteous inherit the earth
Drink now of the eternal sacrament…"

Emile wasn't sure he'd ever been more relieved as he passed through the door to the Sentimental Dead. The calming atmosphere of his favorite place soothed his anxious thoughts. Even though he had known what was going to happen to Branswick ahead of time, the whole experience left him feeling sad and uncomfortable. Foxxe had filled him in on just enough information, sure. But seeing it in person was different. Emile had watched Branswick transform from a sarcastic bastard to a broken and beaten being in a matter of minutes. And while Emile had done this plenty of times before, this experience was different. Knowing the aftermath of their visit was not a good feeling.

Emile walked to the bar and ordered his drink numbly, zoning out to the hubbub around him. Any thought of conversation had left him and he stared blankly ahead.

"What, no witty banter this time?" Morgan asked, sounding bored.

"Not tonight," Emile replied quietly.

Morgan looked at Emile curiously before making his drink. They slid the frothy drink across the smooth surface. Emile grabbed it delicately, as if afraid the glass would shatter within his grip.

"It's on the house tonight. Come back next time with something clever."

Emile smiled tiredly and raised his glass. He wasn't sure if he'd ever feel clever again.

Down the ways from Squall's usual table came Stylos' booming laughter. As Emile walked over, he heard the enthusiastic vampire relaying his latest blight takedown to a group of wide-eyed listeners. They all leaned in, eagerly taking in his fantastic story.

"There I was," Stylos said, waving his hand across the room. "All alone and staring down one of the biggest blight bastards I've ever seen. It had to be over twelve feet tall, long muscular arms ending in sharp claws, with a third one sticking out the back. He smelled like a dead corpse left too long in the hot sun and his cries were thunderous and mighty, shaking the ground beneath us." He stopped and took a drink, savoring the concoction before continuing. "But no blight has ever scared me away, so I stood my ground and bellowed back, 'Come and get me you bloody demon! Come and show me what you've got!'

"Down it came, stomping across the earth. I grabbed my blade and charged right back. It swung at me with its right arm, but I jumped across the decaying limb and severed it at the shoulder. I tumbled, landing on my feet and caught the second arm swinging at me, black blood spraying everywhere. I dodged underneath and took the opportunity to slash open the chest as I dove around."

Emile leaned against a beam and listened, intrigued as the animated monster slayer continued his story.

"It was a nice clean cut, exposing that ugly, mangled heart. I thought to myself, 'This was an easy kill. One more quick slash and I'll have that blackened beast in my hands.' But I'd forgotten about that third arm hanging out the back, and it snatched me round the throat, catching me in the air, my legs dangling like a helpless wee babe. In the panic, I dropped my blade, wrestling with the blight as I struggled to breathe, its giant claws slowly suffocating the life out of me. I swear to this day, I saw the glee in its giant red eye as it watched the life begin to leave mine. But I wasn't to be done in just yet! I grabbed my trusty dagger from my boot." He paused and showed them the dagger nestled into the cuff of his boot. "I grabbed it and jammed it into the blight's wrist, and it dropped me, screaming a horrible unholy shriek. The kind of scream that haunts a being's dreams for all eternity. I took the moment, grabbed my fallen blade and severed the heart from its wailing body. It fell, a corpse and a monster, and I stood, heart in hand, black blood pooling down my arm, chest heaving as I screamed victorious into a clouded sky." Stylos finished his epic tale, fist and eyes to the ceiling, a fired gaze lighting his dark eyes.

Foxxe had joined the listeners silently and looked on, amused. He caught the eye of Stylos, who was basking in the adoration of his listeners, and raised his glass. "Seems like every time I hear you tell that story, it gets an extra arm."

Stylos raised his glass as well and then addressed his adoring fans.

"Don't mind Foxxe here, he's just a bit salty because I've taken more blights down than he has. Now I know it's fun swapping stories of our bloodthirsty escapades, and I'm sure each one of you has some stories worth telling. But my friend here has graciously offered to pay for my drinks tonight, so I think I ought to spend some time thanking him and reminiscing about our olden days together!"

The other vamps looked disappointed but said their goodbyes and departed to the other end of the bar, commenting to each other their thoughts and opinions on taking down blights. Emile watched them pass, wondering how they'd feel if they had to face an actual one and not just listen to Stylos's exciting anecdote. He sat down across from Stylos, while Foxxe took his place at the end of the table.

"Enjoying yourself, I see," Foxxe commented. "How many blended brandies are you in?"

"Enough to feel good, not too many to feel lost," Stylos replied. "I've taken advantage of your charitable nature, Foxxe. Good thing you're well-to-do."

"When you've lived as long as I have, you learn how to invest and acquire wealth," Foxxe replied.

"So," Stylos replied over his drink. "How did it go? Did Branswick make a good choice this evening?"

"You knew about it?" Emile asked, surprised.

"Indeed I did, lad," Stylos replied. "Who do you think set up the compound so it was only Foxxe's friends on duty? Not to mention rescuing that little girl and her mum?"

"You're a very good actor," Emile replied. "At headquarters it was like you hadn't seen each other in a very long time."

"Most things are an act," Foxxe replied. "At least in environments where you're not sure who is being paid off by whom. And yes, he did make a good choice this evening."

"How did you know he would do it?" Emile asked.

"Branswick was many things, but he did love his daughter, in his own messed-up way of loving. Couldn't be there for her in life but at least he was in death."

"To Branswick." Stylos raised his cup.

"To Branswick," Emile and Foxxe repeated, raising their own and taking a swallow.

"Off to Moon City, are you?" Stylos asked. "Wish I could join you. It's been a while since I've been in that blessed city. Used to visit some very lovely ladies there."

"You have lived a charmed life haven't you, Stylos?" Foxxe chuckled. "You always did know how to live the very best even among the worst."

"What's the point of being nearly immortal if you can't enjoy it?" Stylos replied.

"Fair point," Foxxe answered. "Here's to you, Stylos. May we ever be as the gods we claim to be."

The three of them raised their glasses and soberly took another drink. Emile placed his hand on his chest as the fluttering sensations set in again. He was unsettled to find that they reminded him of Link. He wondered briefly if Link ever felt the same.

"If we find what we're looking for in Moon City, we'll be able to get some actual footing on these vampire rogues and maybe even get some insight into these spontaneous blights," Foxxe said.

"That would be nice." Stylos grunted. "Tempest had a blight encounter in our territory to the west. We lost a lot of our human counterparts during that. It's shaken their faith in us, and it was a hell of a reminder what our turned have lingering in their genetics. But Foxxe, it's not just vampires disturbing resource centers. Rogue humans have been at it too."

"So I've heard," Foxxe mused. "I can't say I'm surprised though. There have always been vampire hunters among the humans. They've just changed tactics."

"Vampire hunters?" Emile asked. "Those are still a thing? I thought those were just stories from back in the day."

"Every story has a little bit of truth to it," Stylos replied. "In this case, a lot of truth. Laws and legislation only go so far, and human on vampire violence happens all the time. Sometimes it's just alleyway confrontations. Sometimes it's a lot more."

"At least there haven't been any public stakings or burnings in the last decade and a half," Foxxe interjected. "That was a morbid affair that was incredibly hard to overcome."

"That's not very long ago," Emile pointed out, thinking what a sheltered life he had been raised in.

"It certainly isn't," Foxxe replied. "But they weren't the only guilty party. Some vampires really took on the mantle of shadowed monster and became frenzied feeders. It was not a good time for anyone. We've worked really hard to create healthy connections and monitor potential harm—on both sides of the fence."

"So this one," Stylos said, changing topics. "Tell me about this one."

Emile looked around and behind himself before realizing who Stylos was referring to. "Me?" he asked, pointing to himself.

"Foxxe tasked you with City Salvatore," Stylos continued. "He's brought you along for Branswick. And, he's let you in on one of his many, many charades."

"Um, I think it's just because I'm a member of his squad," Emile replied. Stylos raised an eyebrow which caused Emile to look over at Foxxe. "Am I missing something?"

"Emile, I think you show a lot of potential," Foxxe replied. "You've been with Squall for a while now, and I think it's time for you to start thinking about what your extended future looks like."

"I'm pretty sure my future looks like Squall," Emile replied.

Foxxe smiled supportively. "No doubt Squall is one of the best squadrons around. I said 'one of,' Stylos. Times are changing and I don't know what the future holds. However, Emile, I think you should be considering what you want out of your life. I've asked you to do different things lately to give you a taste of life outside of blight and rogue hunting. There's a lot more that goes on behind the scenes, and you need to know about it if you're going to command your own squadron someday."

Emile almost spit out his drink. "My own what?! Foxxe, I don't know about all that. I'm still trying to figure myself out, never mind leading anybody else. Have you talked to Ash? Or Violetta?"

"Ash and Violetta have different paths, Emile. They're hunters and they always will be. That's what they are good at and that's what they should be allowed to be good at. But you're not just a hunter, are you?"

Emile was quiet. "I don't know about that."

"I do," Foxxe replied. "Because I'm not just a hunter either. I never cared for the battlefield, never cared for the blight hunting. But I did care for change, for advancement. I cared for purpose and for giving others a fighting chance. The way that I cared inspired others, and I found I could lead people and they would listen. I could unite the most unlikely of people, create clever strategies with minimal violence. I could be controlled chaos. Chaos is necessary but it doesn't have to be evil."

"I've never thought of myself as a leader," Emile replied honestly. "I've spent my life following Ash."

"Following Ash and navigating him out of bad situations. Taking the time to evaluate every alternative position before engaging. You can hold your own, Emile. I've watched you do it.

"All I'm saying," Foxxe continued. "Is to think about what you want beyond Squall. If Squall is it, that's fine, but I think you're capable of more. Think on it. I think it's time you came out of the shadows."

Foxxe and Stylos whiled away the following hours recounting war stories, youthful pranks, and Stylos' charismatic and love life. Emile quietly sipped his drink, contemplating Foxxe's words. He'd resigned himself a long time ago to follow Ash to the ends of the earth. He'd never dared think of a life outside of hunting. It *was* enticing.

"I was up by City Salvatore on my way in, by the way." Stylos's voice broke through and Emile's ears perked up. "That blood bank is coming along beautifully. They've even got the vampire community started a little far out to the east of the city. I hear they're looking for a squadron to set up shop in the area . . ."

Stylos' voice drifted back out as Emile pondered the idea of having his own squadron and how odd he felt wanting to ask Link if he could make City Salvatore his home base.

Chapter Eight
"So that the bondage of bone
May be replaced by the freedom of blood..."

"Ash and Emile will go to Lordestowne and take care of the blight there. Violetta and Annora will head to Ravania, and I will go south to Luxeville. We will regroup in Gardovia."

"Why Gardovia?" Violetta asked, swooping her blond curls.

Foxxe took a deep breath. "I have reason to suspect. . . ."

He was cut off by Ash's abrupt entrance.

"It's the blood bank you were at," he yelled, "there's a blight there!"

"Impossible, there was no sign of activity anywhere near that area!" Annora replied, dismayed.

"Dammit," Foxxe interjected. "Go, we have to go now!"

Emile ran with the others, loading quickly into their vehicles and rushing to the scene. His mind was a mess. How could there be a blight at the command center? They had just been there! His thoughts jumped to Commander Hoyt and his Vampire Legionnaires. They had to save them. They had to!

Screams shredded through the air as they entered the compound. Sounds of explosions and the firing of bullets sent a shock of terror through Emile's heart. Bodies of soldiers littered the area, blood pooling and staining the ground around them. Squall raced through, checking for any survivors. They came across a wounded soldier, his abdomen sliced and bleeding heavily.

"Please," he whispered. "Please help me."

Foxxe knelt down and surveyed the damage. Little bits of intestines poked through the openings as the soldier's body shook from pain and shock.

"I'm so sorry," Foxxe said quietly. In a matter of moments, the shaking stopped and the light in the soldier's eyes left. Emile was surrounded by death in his profession, but he never could get used to it. Especially that final moment when you could see life leave the eyes.

A ring of shots sounded out of the darkness from the far southern end of the compound, and the company raced toward it. Rounding a corner, they found Commander Hoyt and his legionnaires holding ground and firing upon the massive beast.

Much like death, blights were something Emile would never get used to. Each manifested a little differently, but all were gruesome in their horrifying transformation. Decaying flesh, additional limbs, swollen eyes, often covered in lumps and oozing sores, blights were lumbering giants of wanton destruction. It towered before the soldiers, flesh hanging from its limbs exposing raw muscles and bones. One eye had fallen from its socket and dangled, swinging side to side as the creature took in its prey. Easily over twelve feet and reeking of rotting flesh, it pawed the ground anxiously, slightly staggering on its sickle-hocked legs. There. That was its weakness.

With a rage-fueled growl, the blight slammed its fists into a nearby vehicle, propelling it toward the gunning soldiers. They deftly scattered and regrouped as Commander Hoyt shouted orders, directing his men. Emile knew he was trying to slow it down, but the best way to take down a blight was either decapitation or removal of the heart. The heart, now grossly enlarged, bulging between splayed ribs, was pulsing against the decaying skin. This was a vampire at its full power, its full potential. Monstrous strength with an unparalleled bloodlust. Terrifying. The thing of nightmares even the most evil of men wouldn't want to dream.

Foxxe signaled the company to move in. Ash and Emile would distract and tank, Annora and Violetta would cripple, and Foxxe would dive for the killing blow. It wasn't too late.

But it was. As the company bounded toward the blight, it released its battle cry and dove into the fray. Bodies of decapitated and half-eaten soldiers flew from the frenzy, the smell of blood both intoxicating and overwhelming, drenched in the scent of fear and pain. Emile and Ash broke through the chaos, slicing at the hanging folds along the blight's body. Guns had no place here, only the true, hard edge of unforgiving steel. The rest of the soldiers ran at the sight of the company and Emile scanned the area, looking for Commander Hoyt. One of the fleeing men caught his eye and, seeming to know what Emile sought, looked upward.

No. Emile turned in horror and slowly lifted his eyes. Time slowed around him; voices became unintelligible as he found the commander hanging limp from the blight's claws as it feasted on his bloodied body. The commander's face fell toward him, pale, his eyes glazed and devoid of life as his entrails fell forward and framed his face. *Too late.* Emile would have cried if he could, but it was too late, it was too far gone. He forced himself back to the present, feeling numb from shock.

Behind the blight, Annora and Violetta sliced the tendons in his ankles, forcing him to his knees. Emile could hear the cackling from Violetta and spied her dancing between the blight's legs. Her blond hair was matted in black blood, dripping down across her pale face. But her eyes were gleeful and she smiled a crazed grin as she sliced away.

From the building behind, Vaughn Foxxe launched himself from the roof, two steel spears in his hands. He landed square against the blight, the spears driving through the chest and into the ground. Pinned. With quick work he drew his knife and carved out the heart while the blight screamed and writhed. Emile and Ash hacked the arms off at the shoulder to keep it from clawing Vaughn, and within a few moments, the screeching ceased, and Vaughn tossed the oozing black heart into the dirt beside them.

Emile looked to the body of the commander, now on his side, facing away. He wanted to go to him, wanted to fix it, to apologize, to do *something*. *Anything*. But he stood where he was and watched the remaining soldiers cover the mangled body.

"Where did it come from?" Annora asked, her blades sticky with blood, her face drenched in sweat and dirt.

"This isn't the first one that has popped out of the blue," Foxxe said. "My companion in the next district says there've been incidents. No warning, just immediate destruction. No vampire has ever mutated that quickly. *Never.* Something is grossly wrong and it's happening at a terrifying rate. Complete peace and then without a warning ultimate destruction."

"Maybe someone is dropping them off," Ash surmised.

"But how could anyone be controlling or containing these things?" Violetta asked. "You'd have to have a hefty cargo container to haul them and that'd be pretty noticeable. And traceable."

"That's why we're going to Gardovia," Foxxe replied. "There are elite vampires defecting and disappearing. There are some camping out in Moon City waiting to pass over. Plus, whoever is sending out the rogue vampires has been hiring them out of there. We're going to go there and find out."

"Moon City!" Ash and Violetta murmured in tandem. Besides Foxxe and Annora, none of them had been to the legendary city. Hidden deep in the forests of Gardovia, Moon City was a haven for all enchanted and unique creatures. A haven if you were on the run. A good place to disappear and come out as someone or something new. Or a good place to dig a grave for a fee.

Emile would have been excited had it not been for the carnage he was standing in, his own hands caked in drying blight blood. He caught a look at his reflection, and he didn't like what he saw. An inhuman creature caked in blood, holding weapons still dripping, eyes seething with rage and disgust. A monster. How long until he became a blight? Would he feel the change?

Reinforcements had arrived on the scene, as well as the containment crew who began cleaning up the space, assessing damage and tending to survivors. This blight had taken out over half of the compound on its way through. This wouldn't be an easy cleanup. The air around Emile hung heavy with cries of the wounded, blood and fear still coating the breeze. He forced himself to walk to Commander Hoyt's body and knelt down next to him. Emile would not cry. He could not. But he knelt there in the destruction by the man who had given him a second chance. A human man who had faith in the inhuman.

And now a dead man, laid to waste by the very thing he once trusted.

Emile was still staring at the commander's covered body when Ash laid a soft hand on his shoulder. He didn't speak but Emile knew he too grieved. Emile had been closer to the commander, but Hoyt had always looked out for Ash as well. Whether he was caught sneaking in liquor, picking fights, or parading around with the newest pretty girl he had acquired, Hoyt knew how to handle Ash and his wild ways. Ash was the instigator, Emile the quiet follower, and somehow the commander had found ways to protect, guide, and grow them. Hoyt didn't back down when he was ridiculed as a vampire lover. When his friends in high places took advantage of his Vampiric Legionnaires as proof that working relations with vampires took away from human needs and human military objectives. He was proud of his work bringing peace between species. He was proud of his title. He was proud of Ash and Emile. And now he was dead, slain by the thing Emile would one day become. That he and Ash would both become. And for a moment, he couldn't deny the admiral's sneer, and in his mind, he echoed the label of a rabid, feral creature.

Chapter Nine

"Oh sisters, oh brothers, do not dismay
Do not despair even unto the end of night..."

The next day peaked early and Ash and Emile were both in aggravated moods. Emile still felt the rage of yesterday's kill and Ash wasn't far from it himself. It didn't help matters that Ash wasn't really about mornings to begin with.

Today they'd be headed for Lordestowne to find the blight, end it, and piece together any information they could find. Emile downed his breakfast while watching his favorite show of genetically mutated creatures that saved the world. He could not help but see himself reflected in the characters. Leftover reruns from the old world. From before the world.

Ash downed his drink and shoved on his boots. "You ready to go hunting, brother?" He smiled wickedly.

"Always."

"Good. But I'm driving."

"You always get to drive!"

"I know." Ash grinned and sauntered out the door. It would take them most of the day to get to Lordestowne, and Emile was not particularly excited about getting there. Lordestowne was notorious for one thing and one thing only: feeders. Since vamps couldn't get high the normal way, they took to feeding on drugged humans. In Lordestowne, an elite ran the vampire blood ring. If you were a human in need of services or money, you could exchange your blood. It involved copious, and sometimes lethal, amounts so only the very desperate could be found in their circle. Some humans who were lost to that lifestyle lived out their days there, rotating feeds. Officials had attempted to outlaw the blood prostitution, but the elites were powerful and wealthy. Enough bribes left their little town undisturbed. The fact that a blight was prowling an area heavily populated by vampires seemed ridiculous—it was blood the beasts called after.

But maybe business had been good lately, Emile thought, recalling the uptick in missing humans.

Vincent Valkane, the elite running the blood and drug circle, had not deigned Foxxe worthy of replies or information, regardless of Foxxe's request. Elites in general often felt they were above the laws of man and beast, powerful and free to do as they wished. But Valkane had no interest in politics beyond the persuasion necessary to secure his own wealth and stability. Or so it was said. Some said he was mad. Emile was inclined to believe it.

"Are you doing okay since . . .yesterday?" Ash asked, cautiously.

"Yeah, I'm fine."

There was silence and Ash said, "It'd be okay if you weren't fine."

. Emile sat quietly and then replied, "It doesn't really matter if I'm fine because the whole world is going to keep on going. It doesn't matter that we were late to the attack, it doesn't matter that the commander is dead, because everything is just going to keep on going regardless. As if it never happened, as if . . .as if he never lived and those men never lived. Like there's barely a difference.'

"Oh, there's a difference," Ash replied. "And the world is a worse place without him in it. For all the stupid shit I did, he treated me well and punished me even better and pushed me to be more. And you, well, he looked after you damn well."

"Yeah, he did."

"Do you remember that time I got shit-faced and one of the privates dared me to wake up the wolfhounds?"

"Yes, I do, and you did, and you almost died!"

"Yeah, it was a good time. I had such an adrenaline rush! But afterward Commander Hoyt took me aside and asked me what my problem was and why was I doing this to my family."

"Your family?" Emile questioned, knowing neither of them had one.

"Yeah, you, dumbass. He said if kept doing things like that I'd get myself or you killed or maimed, and how would it be if I left you alone?"

"I'd be fine," Emile retorted.

"No, you wouldn't." Ash laughed. "You'd be lost, alone, and spend the rest of your life brooding in an abandoned church."

"You're an ass."

"I am delightful," Ash replied. A few minutes later he added, "But it's the same for you, you know. I'd be lost without you."

"Yeah, I know. I'm pretty delightful too."

They spent the rest of their journey reminiscing over the commander and their days in the military. Emile laughed and *almost* cried and even though it hurt, it made the commander feel alive. And Emile realized it had meant something. And it could still mean something if he chose to believe it. So he did.

He pondered on the thoughts of family as Ash settled into his favorite rock and roll, casually smoking out the window, the butt gracefully perched between his fingers in their fingerless gloves. Emile closed his eyes and allowed himself a dip into his memory. He could vaguely hear his mother laughing, feel her soft hand against his cheek. Smell the fresh bread she was always making and hear his father laughing as he stole slices of peppers she had chopped for dinner. He fondly remembered his sister. She was so young, just reaching eight the last time . . . the last time he had seen her.

"The past doesn't matter anymore." Violetta's words echoed in his mind. Her whole story rattled in his brain. He understood what she meant when she said it. He heard the conviction in her voice. Saw it, in the steadiness of her knife. But it still felt wrong. It felt wrong to act like the memories of his family no longer mattered. *"Examine your choices in the present,"* she had told him. Emile wasn't sure what that meant. Choices? For his entire turned existence he had followed Ash. Wherever Ash went, there was Emile. They were always together, fighting together, living life together, arguing together. Emile was grateful for the life he had, he was glad to be part of something good. But had he chosen it? Not really. He had just fallen into it, following Ash as he always did. So who was he? Was he a victor and protector

of the people? Or just a monster lurking in the shadows, too afraid to accept what he was?

And then there was Foxxe's proposal. Become a leader, maybe even have his own squad. The more Emile thought about it, the more he warmed to the idea. He still hadn't told Ash about his conversation with Foxxe, and part of him felt guilty for it. He'd always told Ash everything. He wondered what Ash would think about this life change, and he wondered more if Ash would follow him as he had always followed Ash.

He leaned over to switch the station and Ash swatted his hand.

"Stop touching," Ash growled. "Driver picks the music."

"Driver can kindly mind his own business. It's a long drive and I'm tired of screeching guitars."

Ash rolled his eyes but said nothing. Emile knew Ash was letting him have this one.

The ride was uneventful, much to Emile's relief. They arrived at dusk, checking into the reservations Foxxe had made for them at a local motel. It lay outside the city, small and unnoticeable, slightly peeling blue paint framing old windows. Emile supposed it wasn't important enough to warrant attention from the lord of Lordestowne. They each grabbed their bags and checked in to their room. The vampire behind the desk looked up over her book, thick black glasses perched on the edge of her nose.

"Don't make a mess or you'll be charged. Any Nutrimentum you consume is an additional cost. If you bring any *guests* back please be discreet. Check out is dusk. Oh, I see you don't have a designated checkout day. Well when you do, it's dusk. If you have any questions ask someone else because I'm busy."

"Thank you," Emile replied, unsure of how to respond. The vampire just looked at him and then disappeared into the back office.

"What a delightful host," Ash commented as they walked to their room. "I suppose I can't blame her though. After all, look at this place."

He pushed open the door to their room. Twin beds covered in dusty blue blankets that had seen some time, old wallpaper slightly peeling in the corners decorated in gaudy gold roses and thick black stripes. The double window was covered by ebony velvet drapes with gold tassels and trim. A worn-out cooler hummed in the background, further adding to the ambience.

"At least it's clean," Emile offered. "I know Valkane offered nicer residence farther into the city when he heard we were coming, but I really didn't want to stay there."

"The sooner we can get done and leave, the better," Ash pointed out, settling onto his bed. He reached into his bag and pulled out a tube of Nutrimentum. He gave it a couple quick shakes before snapping the top off and guzzling it down. "The best thing they did when they made this was the self-heating bit," he said. "Can't imagine drinking it cold."

Emile pulled his own tube out and observed it, the contents swirling form side to side. It had the consistency and look of blood but smelled and tasted completely different. Emile tried not to drink straight blood when he could. It gave him flashbacks to his early days as a turned. In the fevers of his infection when he'd lost control and . . . He shook his tube, sparking the reactive ingredients into action. It grew warm in his palm, and he popped the cap and swallowed. It would do until they absolutely had to feed again.

"Well, this is exciting," Ash said.

Emile rolled onto his side and said, "Sorry you're stuck with me. I know I'm not the company you'd usually prefer."

Ash just grumbled from his bed, face down in the pillows.

Emile thought silently for a moment before saying, "I bet if Violetta were here instead of me, you'd be in a much better mood."

Ash lifted up and narrowed his eyes. "I don't know what you mean."

Emile cocked his head and smiled. "Oh I think you do. Always offering to go on recon with her every chance you get. Teasing her incessantly about her looks just to get under her skin. You like pissing her off. And she likes getting pissed off."

Ash dropped his demeanor and shrugged nonchalantly, falling back onto the bed. "Violetta could have anyone she wants."

"I wondered what happened when the girls stopped coming over and you cleaned up your act."

"Maybe I just got tired. Maybe I grew up."

"Or maybe you fell in loooooove," Emile crooned. "Violetta is pretty badass. You'd be suited to each other."

"Yeah well, she's not interested in me, so. It ain't gonna happen."

"Poor Ash, forever alone." Emile sighed. "Maybe I'll ask her out."

Ash opened one eye. "I'd like to see you try."

"Is that a dare?"

"A warning. She's handy with those knives. Violetta may be a tease but that's all she is. That's why I keep my distance. I don't know where she came from, but I never got the vibe it was somewhere nice."

Emile contemplated. On one hand he was surprised Ash didn't know, but on the other hand . . . "Why is it so hard and weird to ask other turned how they came to be?"

"Because it might be traumatic and terrible, and we don't want to make them relive it. Or it might be a regret or a mistake. Or maybe they asked for it and we all know how you feel about that."

"Well," he said slowly, "my feelings on that have changed."

"How interesting," Ash replied, sitting up. "Why?"

"I just . . . I've started to see things a little bit differently. Listen, I've lived most of my turned life very angry and resentful of people who made this choice themselves because I never got to. I never had a say. I just woke up like this one day and that was that. But I think I'm beginning to realize that it doesn't really matter how we end up here, it's about how we deal with it afterward. Some beings look at this like it's a second chance, and I can't begrudge them that."

"Geez Mr. Positivity, what'd you do with Emile?" Ash replied sarcastically, but Emile could tell he was pleased.

"I'm just trying to be more focused on here and now."

"Don't focus too hard. Those gilded roses and black stripes will haunt your dreams," Ash replied. "But seriously, I'm glad to hear it. It's taken you long enough."

"Ash, do you remember during my fevers ... when I attacked our neighbor who came to check on me?"

"Yes," Ash replied very quietly.

"I knew who she was when it happened. I knew and yet somehow it just didn't matter. I saw her and just ... wanted to consume her. Every last drop. If you hadn't arrived when you did, I would have."

Ash listened quietly as Emile continued.

"When we fight the blights, that's all I see. Myself as a monster devouring everything in sight. As if I have no control and everything around me is a temporary stasis before I lose my grip and devour my neighbors."

"Emile, there's no way of knowing if or when you might turn into a blight," Ash countered. "I know the transition is horrible. I remember what it was like when I went through mine. And Emile, I did kill beings during mine."

"You never told me that."

Ash sighed. "I was angry and upset about it for a long time, but eventually I realized that what happened wasn't something I could have stopped. I had no one helping me, I had no understanding of what was happening. Do I regret it? Of course I do. But what can I do about it? Not a damn thing. You have to forgive yourself eventually, Emile, otherwise your life is a waste."

"And you've forgiven yourself?" Emile asked.

"For some things," Ash replied. "But not everything," he added softly.

"All those pretty hearts you've broken along the way, no doubt," Emile teased.

"Listen, I can't help that I'm a beautiful man that the lovely ladies flock to," he replied defensively.

"And yet, here you are, in a hotel room with me and no lovely ladies. Or Violetta. So sad." He mournfully placed his hand across his heart. "To the handsome man that was."

Ash whipped a pillow at him, and they both laughed. It felt good to laugh. For the first time in a long while, he felt a little lighter. He could almost have sworn that his heart beat a little faster.

"Okay, time to sleep," Ash said. "Tomorrow we start the hunt and talk to Valkane."

"Cannot *wait* for that," Emile replied, throwing himself back onto his pillow. "I've heard a lot of things about Valkane. He's ruthless, extremely intelligent, handsome, and smooth."

"He's exceptionally smooth," Ash answered. "He can make you believe anything if you listen long enough. Elites are dangerous when they feel safe and comfortable, and this man has built himself a kingdom where he's untouchable. His power is persuasion. Not like Annora's where it's commanding, but more suggestive. He whispers in ears and makes sly comments, convincing you that you thought of his grand scheme. It's just one of the many ways he controls people."

"Are you going to be all right being here, Ash?"

"Yes. The past was a long time ago, and the one who turned me is dead now. Just don't believe what he tells you, about anything. He can't be trusted."

Emile nodded. Ash knew this town best. He'd grown up on the city's dirty streets. He shuddered when he thought about what his life must have been like. Emile knew tomorrow they'd start the hunt and get the answers they were looking for.

The last thing Emile saw was Ash lighting a cigarette.

Chapter Ten

"For where the light has abandoned
Shadows will spring forth to enshroud us..."

The next morning was overcast and Emile was grateful for the cloudy weather. It seemed wrong to have a sunny day after all that had transpired. He and Ash had been up early scouting the city. Foxxe may have told Valkane they were here for the blight, but Ash and Emile were doing some undercover work as well.

"Don't bring attention to yourselves," Foxxe said. "Make it look like you're examining traffic ways and breaches where the blight can enter the city and do the most damage. But listen. Listen carefully. Elites have a bad habit of sharing important secrets with their blood companions."

In Lordestowne sat an unfettered den of iniquity. The elites here, as well as well-to-do turned, lived in the center of the city, in vast lavish mansions that spoke of money and sin. Ornate brass gates separated them from the lesser vampires and humans. Those lesser creatures lived in, not quite slums, but starkly lacking the ornate gates, manicured lawns, and newest models of transportation. In a world decimated by war and grief, it made Emile cringe to see such wanton abuse and misuse of vampiric power.

Ash and Emile spent the day learning the layout of the city. They'd walked the perimeter and found the least protected entry points. Valkane may have guarded his kingdom to the teeth, but there were always weaknesses if you knew where and how to look. The boys had only run into a few people and some vampires on the way for a feed on humans drugged up on gods knew what. The vamps on the way to feed were impatient and easily aggravated. The few times Ash and Emile stopped to ask questions they were met with subdued violence—bared fangs and explosive attitudes. They had let the vamps pass, hands in the air, mouths closed.

"Don't interrupt a vamp on the way to their feed," Ash remarked. "Especially crazy ones like these."

The humans they ran into were mostly unresponsive, though a few were chattering excitedly.

"My feeder always gets the good stuff," a particularly vocal girl had told Emile. "Quick feed and I'll be on my way. On my way back home. Good pay today, good pay. I'll be good for a while. Less mouths to feed at home anyway since my uncle went missing. Ran out on his family. Bastard! That's okay, who needs him? Gods I'm hungry." She continued to ramble as they wound through the city.

"Does this bother you?" Emile asked softly.

"It's not great, but it's fine," Ash replied. "It's not all bad you know. Vamps consume quickly, and then there are only trace amounts left in the bloodstream. The effects wear off with minimal damage. And most feeders, especially here, pay handsomely."

"Surely you're not defending this after what happened to you?"

"No!" Ash said quickly, "But many of these people are just trying to survive. Even some of the vamps are just trying to survive. I don't think it's right—I think it's wrong! There are better ways but . . . I was one of them once, so I remember what it was like."

"Your parents sold you into it. It's not like you had a choice."

Ash was quiet and Emile was worried he had gone too far when they were interrupted by a swarthy vamp covered in tattoos. He stepped into their path, arms crossed, blocking their way.

"Master Valkane requests your presence this evening for dinner," he stated, his deep voice echoing in the alleyway.

"We've been expecting an invitation," Ash replied.

"Which we will be happy to oblige," Emile interjected, sensing Ash's irritation.

"Be at his residence by seven o'clock. The guards will let you in." With that, the messenger departed into the shadows.

"Did you see the muscles on that guy?" Emile squeaked. "Is that the kind of vampire that Valkane surrounds himself with?"

"Wouldn't you?" Ash replied. "For all his power, Valkane is still a businessman with some hefty sins to answer for. Only the best of the best would be surrounding me if I were him."

They continued on in silence, Ash puffing on his cigarette, his face cloudy.

"Do you ever think of where you might be if you hadn't . . . hadn't been sold here?" Emile asked.

"Not really. Honestly, it was the best thing that could have happened to me considering where I came from. I would have died eventually; it was just a matter of time."

"You're still gonna die anyway. We both are. And it ain't gonna be pretty."

"No," Ash said. "But at least I have a choice. And," he added, "I can smoke as much as I want." He winked and lit another cigarette, letting it hang lazily between his lips.

"Nasty habit," Emile replied sticking his nose in the air.

"Says the vamp who still tries it to 'look cool,'" Ash replied, shoving Emile's shoulder.

"Ohhh, I am not looking forward to tonight," Emile said. "I haven't been around many elites. They always make me feel a little unsettled."

"To be expected since they are so superior and perfect in every way," Ash mocked.

"That's right, say more clever things that definitely won't get us killed," Emile retorted.

"Oh, look at me, I'm an elite." Ash puffed out his chest and walked pompously around. "I can do anything I want, and all will bow before me."

Emile stifled a laugh. "We best go get cleaned up. We want to represent our company well tonight."

Ash bowed and gestured for Emile to lead the way and then sauntered down the road, hands in pocket, a new cigarette hanging from his mouth. *The best thing that could have ever happened.* It echoed in Emile's mind and he couldn't help but selfishly feel it that Ash's turning had been the best thing for him too.

A quick clean up and clothes change had them looking dapper and respectable—a perfect image of professional killers for hire. *Well, blight killers,* Emile thought. He wore his best—dark slacks, his black leather vest, and a navy blue button-up shirt beneath. Collared shirts always made him feel stifled, and he haphazardly rolled his sleeves to the elbow. He tried fixing his hair but the comb could only do so much. He tucked it behind his ears and hoped for the best. Ash still wore his navy blue coat with brass buttons, but underneath he was dressed in black pants, a black striped vest, and a silken black shirt, open at the collar. His messy black hair was gathered in a stubby ponytail at his neck, a few of his unruly hairs falling and framing his face. And of course, that infernal cigarette hanging between his full lips.

Emile narrowed his eyes. *Always has to one up me,* he thought. But he supposed that was how Ash always managed with the ladies. Who can resist a ruggedly handsome man with secrets and possible bloodlust?

Emile attempted to smooth his hair one more time before giving up, and they headed out of the hotel.

A shiny black car rolled up in front of them, the front window sliding down.

"Master Valkane sends his regards," a voice called from inside, "and sent his car to fetch you."

Emile and Ash exchanged glances.

"Thanks, but we'll walk," Emile replied.

"Master Valkane won't appreciate ungrateful guests," the voice crooned. "Especially as he hopes to work with your esteemed Foxxe and company."

Ash rolled his eyes. "Fine."

The window slid up as Ash and Emile crawled into the back. The back of the car was spacious, decked in supple black leather, light jazz playing on the stereo. It made Emile think of the Sentimental Dead, and he suddenly wished he was home. Across from the boys sat two human girls. They both looked nervous.

"Why are you here?" Ash asked.

"We're . . . we're here for you," one girl replied nervously, her eyes darting between them. "Master Valkane thought you might . . . want some refreshment."

"We don't feed from humans," Emile gently reassured them. "But we will tell your master that you were good hosts."

The girls visibly relaxed, leaning into each other.

"You work for Valkane?"

"We belong. We were bargained to him for the safety of our families."

"What kind of drugs does he have you on?" Ash asked.

"None. He likes our blood pure and untainted. It is a kindness."

Emile bit back the words lingering in his throat. *A kindness.* Ash, ever the charmer, had the girls giggling by the time they arrived at Valkane's home, and even Emile had leaned in, awkwardly flirting with the brunette. It felt good to just *exist.* But the chatter quieted as they rolled past the bronze gates and into the home of Vincent Valkane.

The mansion sat back from the road and gleaming brass gates, surrounded by vast gardens with delicately trimmed topiaries and dotted with trailing flowers and blossoming trees. Emile took in the beauty, a stark contrast to the being it housed. The house was a massive, sprawling work of art. A foundation of white stonework was interrupted by massive domed windows framed in sparkling gilding. Carvings of angels and goddesses were sprinkled through the gardens, framed by massive white pillars leading into the entrance. Stark white steps carried them to the threshold of massive double doors. A human servant stood present and ushered them through the doors.

"I never took Valkane for such . . . beautiful tastes," Emile commented.

"Master Valkane prefers being surrounded by beautiful things," one of the girls replied.

Emile swallowed the bile in his throat, fully noting the beauty of the girls. Of course. He wondered briefly what happened when Valkane's captives were no longer beautiful but shoved the thoughts down, unable to look the girls in the face.

The staircase was long and impressive, and Emile suspected it was partly like that to intimidate the beings entering Valkane's home. He passed through the double doors and stopped short once inside, bombarded by the many mirrors decorating the walls. Mirrors of every shape and size, some borderline garish, lined the entryway and continued into the vast expanse interrupted by twin staircases trimmed in mahogany leading to the second floor.

"What is up with these mirrors?" Emile asked. "Kinda creepy."

"Like she said, he loves being surrounded by beauty," Ash replied, eyeing the area. "Both himself and others."

"Ash Crosse and Emile Thorne. Welcome to my home. So gracious of you to accept my invitation." A smooth, almost silvery voice floated from atop the staircase. Vincent Valkane. Emile had heard of the beautiful, vile creature before him, but the descriptions hadn't done him justice. Valkane began his descent, his movements graceful, almost liquid. He was tall and lithe with an air of fragility that Emile suspected betrayed his true strength and prowess. His long blond hair was unbound, perfectly smooth, gleaming in the light of the crystal chandeliers. Emile could not believe that this angelic being was the mastermind behind the infamous Lordestowne.

"Please, allow me to introduce myself, formally. Vincent Valkane, Esquire, at your assistance." He bowed before taking Emile's hand. His hands were smooth, as though they had never worked, his nails perfectly manicured, and his fingers caressed in numerous rings bedecked in gold and precious gems. Emile was not sure he had ever seen a more beautiful creature, with flawless pale skin and an unnatural presence . . . until Emile locked eyes with him.

Dead eyes. Soulless, black, dead eyes. Emile started back and Valkane cocked his head, smiling around his expressionless eyes, but said nothing in response.

Coyly, Valkane directed his attention to Ash.

"Ash," he practically purred. "So long since I've been graced with your presence. Oh how I've missed you," he said, wickedly.

Emile shot Ash a questioning look, but Ash looked bored as he idly lit another cigarette.

Valkane wrinkled his nose. "Still going on with that nasty habit, are you? Only thing that ruins you, Ash darling. That and your insufferable *morals*."

Ash merely shrugged.

"Oh, did you not enjoy these delectable beauties?" Valkane asked, stepping between the girls grasping one by the wrist.

"We don't feed on humans directly. Seems a bit . . . primitive," Ash finally said.

Valkane smiled. "There is beauty even in the primitive. In the animal. In the power of dominance and authority." With that, he swiftly drew the girl's neck to his lips, puncturing her soft flesh and drinking deeply.

"Ahhhh," he said, finished, his white teeth coated in blood. "What a loss."

Not a hair out of place, not a drop of blood on his white velvet vest adorned in gold buttons. Not a hint on his crisp cream shirt, cuffs trimmed in lace. It made Valkane appear even more sinister as he stood smiling while servants rushed the girls away and a servant handed him a ruby kerchief which he daintily tapped his face with. Valkane may have been spotless, but the girl he had feasted on was not. White as death, she clutched a towel to her neck as red slowly seeped through it. She was supported by her sister as they disappeared up the staircase, no doubt to change their dresses freckled in blood and beautify themselves for their master.

"Come," Valkane said, turning on his heel. "Let us dine and chat." He led the way to the left and into a large room painted sky blue with white trim, each corner supported by a white pillar. More mirrors lined the walls, and Valkane sat at the head of a long mahogany table decked in gold silverware and porcelain plates. Behind him two bodyguards stood waiting as Ash and Emile sat down beside each other, close to the door.

"I took the liberty of preparing your dinner," he said simply. "Since you prefer that foul concoction of nutrients over the fresh substance." He clicked his fingers and servants appeared, setting down silver goblets filled to the brim.

"Please enjoy." Valkane waved his hand, encouraging them to drink.

Emile looked down into his goblet, unsure if he could stomach the contents. His rage seethed beneath his skin, and he wished for nothing more than to reach across the table and separate Valkane's body from his loathsome, smiling head. But Valkane was protected by the elites, and as long as the humans came and went willingly, Valkane was above the law. And even if they didn't, his power and wealth granted him the blind eyes of equally corrupt officials.

Valkane, he noticed, had no goblet. As if sensing Emile's question Valkane lazily spoke.

"I'm ready for my dinner."

A stunning young man, blond and blue-eyed, stepped forward and Valkane beckoned him into his lap. The young lad tilted his head back as Valkane ran his nose along the throat.

"Mmmmm," he crooned. "Always smells so delightful. A little fear mixed with apprehension." And those cold, dead eyes locked with Emile as he sank his teeth into his meal. The victim closed his eyes as his master fed, the color draining from his face. Emile felt a flash, a sudden pain as if he too felt the life draining from him. And suddenly it was him on Valkane's lap, life leaving him and then . . . and then he was violently jolted back, searing pain in his skull and bones as though he was being broken and remade . . .

Emile closed his eyes and breathed silently, forcing the feeling out of his mind, far, far away where he kept all the dark things that lurked in the shadows of his mind. When he reopened his eyes, Valkane had finished dining and simply sat watching him.

"Curious," he murmured. "You know, Emile, you have such stunning eyes. Like a shining crystal sapphire. Quite beautiful. I'm sure those eyes have gotten you out of some . . . unpleasant situations." He leaned back in his chair, smiling as though he knew something Emile didn't.

"Foxxe sends his regards," Ash interrupted. "And he thanks you for your cooperation as we secure the city and hunt the blight."

"But of course," Valkane said dismissively. "Wouldn't want to cross the almighty Foxxe would I? And someone needs to take care of those wretched creatures. It's not a full blight, hence why it hasn't gone completely savage. We keep tabs on all our workers and feeders as well. It wasn't any of mine that began the transformation. Though I've heard there's been quite the problem with random, fully developed blights popping up."

"I don't suppose you'd know how these wretched creatures are just *popping up* out of nowhere?" asked Emile.

Valkane's eyes narrowed. "No. I wouldn't."

"Must be scary having something so hideous nearby. Is that why you bathe in beauty? Because you know how ugly this world you've built really is?"

Valkane's teeth flashed. "I'd be more respectful in your tone, *boy*."

"Why? Every time you allow your turned friends to feed on some poor, jacked-up human you let them inch a little bit closer."

"Emile," Ash warned.

"No, let your friend speak. I like how his eyes glitter when he's angry." Valkane smiled. "While I have made a wealthy kingdom in this profession of blood bargaining, I myself do not indulge in such base behavior."

"Then why surround yourself with such an ugly thing?"

"Because, dear boy, the destruction that follows is glorious. Life slowly ebbing, a silent destruction. Even death. Beautiful devastation."

"And yet you live in a home decorated in mirrors. Because you're afraid of what might sneak up on you?"

"No," replied Valkane, smiling around those black pits, rising from his chair. "Because I see all and know all. I wasn't the first in this city. There was one before me. But he did it all wrong. He was lazy and sloppy, so I took it from him and made it mine. I built this place into the glory that it is. And it is a glory, whether you see it so or not. I created this from nothing, and I continue to create from nothing. Do you think a vampire like myself would live as long as I have without making sure I know all things at all times?" He leaned into the table. "I. See. Everything. And I. Know. Everything." Something dark and terrifying overcame his countenance and then disappeared as he sat back, seemingly bored and uninterested.

"How long will you be in my city?"

"Just long enough to take out the blight," Ash replied. "Foxxe was wondering if you've noticed any disappearances lately—vamp or otherwise."

Valkane waved his hand. "People come and go all the time; how should I know where they are going. I keep track of the important ones and in my inner circle, none have 'disappeared.'"

"Do you have any other information that may be helpful to us in regard to the blights?" Emile asked impatiently.

"If I did, I'd be more than happy to share the information with you," he replied. "But I have none. So, I suggest you do your job and leave my kingdom."

He rose, dismissing them, and walked out of the room. "My servants will see you out. Lovely to meet you, Emile. And Ash, think about coming home. We miss you. Oh, and Emile"—he paused and looked over his shoulder—"do be careful out there. The past has a way of . . . repeating itself." He flashed a smile and then he was gone.

"What does that mean?" Emile asked as he rose.

"Who knows," Ash responded. "It's Valkane. He talks in circles."

Ash and Emile hurried out the door, the sun setting in the distance. There was no car waiting for them as they marched down the white steps onto the stone driveway. Emile felt as though eyes were boring into him from behind, and when he turned around, he scanned the wide windows and found Valkane watching as they left. He smiled at Emile, and Emile quickly turned and continued his walk through the brass gates. He couldn't place it, but something about Valkane's mirthless stare caused his head to pound, a piercing pressure starting at the base of his skull and radiating to the crown of his head. He tried to shake it off as they left the grounds and continued on their way. Emile glanced at Ash to see if he felt the same, but all he saw was a fresh cigarette and his friend's face folded in quiet sadness.

Nighttime was the best time for taking out a blight. A vampire's senses were enhanced at night, making them faster, more lethal, and precise. Ash and Emile had found it on the outside of the city, taking out the wayward wanderers but never trespassing in. Emile suspected that Valkane's men had kept it from entering to protect his many 'investments' but had made no effort to actually kill it. Leaving it to the professionals, Emile supposed.

While the one at the compound had been long and gangly, mutating with massive strength and extra limbs, this one was short and squat, swaying as it moved. Emile saw what Valkane meant when he had said it wasn't a full blight. Both its size and mutation weren't as far progressed, though it didn't stop the creature from incurring a typical blight's look and smell. The decaying folds of skin were a sickly gray color, mottled with black and green. Its lips were full and bulbous, drool hanging from the jagged teeth. It did not hear the pair approach as it suckled on a deer carcass. A gust of wind blew the blight's scent, and both Ash and Emile gagged.

Everything about a blight was death incarnate. Though all blights maintained a heightened blood lust, ones that weren't fully mutated could be content hunting on animals while the fully morphed, stronger ones, broke through cities and slaughtered the citizens. It all depended on the genetics lying in wait in a vampire's body. Usually there were signs in the lead-up to a vampire becoming a blight—and some chose to end their life early while others rode it out to the last breath. On very rare occasions there were volatile blights—an immediate transformation caused by an extreme trauma that woke the genes up early. It didn't happen often, which made the increased, sporadic appearance of blights ever more mystifying.

Thankfully, this would be an easy kill. Emile and Ash approached slowly and quietly. Ash raised his favorite pistol, aiming for the exposed back. He shot, hitting the blight directly in the center, sending an array of electrical impulses meant to stun and contain. The pair leaped into action. You had to be swift when taking out a blight, but Ash and Emile had worked so long together that they flowed seamlessly, without even needing to speak.

Emile wore studded gloves for close combat, while Ash favored a matching set of swords. He swung them easily, severing the limbs holding the deer carcass. Emile came from the side, slamming his fist into the blight's head, knocking it off balance. As the creature fell, Emile stepped onto its wriggling body, and Ash deftly chopped out the black heart. He tossed it next to the blight and decided to try out a new explosive bullet Foxxe had given him.

"Well, I'd say these new bullets are highly effective," Ash remarked, surveying the scene. Black, bloody bits of blight coated the forest floor, pooling rotting juices.

"Yeah, but now we're coated in this . . . stink," Emile complained and wrinkled his nose. "Gods." He gagged. "At least we don't have to clean this up."

"Nah. It's a nice little present for Valkane's men." Ash holstered his gun, grinning. "It's the least we could do."

"I hope I don't have to see that being again for a long time," Emile replied. "I look forward to the day his sins catch up to him."

"Do you think they will?" Ash asked.

"Of course. These things always do. Are you tired?"

Ash grinned. "You know a good kill always gets the adrenaline going."

"Then let's clean up and get the hell out of here. I don't want to spend another minute in this place."

Ash wiped his face with a handkerchief, removing bits of the blight. "I couldn't agree more. But I'm driving."

"Of course you are," Emile replied as they began their trek to the hotel.

Ash had been quiet during their visit with Valkane, not like his usual bravado. Almost as if he were afraid of something. *That's stupid, Ash isn't afraid of anything,* Emile thought.

Emile wondered if it just brought back bad memories. But a small part of him ached as Valkane's words echoed in his brain. *"Ash, think about coming home. We miss you. Oh, and Emile . . .do be careful out there. The past has a way of repeating itself."* And deep down, in the dark quiet places that held his past, something ached, as though a long-silenced voice was finally trying to scream.

"Ash," Emile said. "I need to stop somewhere before we go home."

Chapter Eleven

"Protection from those who linger
From those who would seek us harm..."

Home

Emile sucked in his breath as they turned off down a dusty dirt road. After deciding to stay the night for some extra rest, they'd left the raucous atmosphere of Lordestowne far behind and found themselves in the quiet glow of farm country. They drove past fallow fields silently resting, and Emile wished for a moment that he was one of them. He recognized these fields and hills—places he had explored and wandered in his youth. He knew the people who lived here, had played with their children, and helped build their barns. It'd been ten years since Emile had been to his family home, and he ached as they drove closer.

Maybe I'm not ready, Emile thought, panic slowly rising in his core. But when his home came into view, everything fell aside, and he knew it was time.

This farming community was a small one. Homesteads were pretty well spread out, and the whole community sat surrounded by thickly wooded forest of evergreens. Emile's family farm sat closest to the tree line, as if it were being gently hugged by nature. He had spent countless hours in those trees. Both he and Ash had, chasing rabbits and shooting arrows, daring each other to climb trees and jump rocks—and then subsequently regretting those dares. The land resting on either side of the house and barn had been plowed and planted, neat rows of leafy green growth promised a good harvest. While Emile had been changing, and Ash was burying his family, he had also signed over the land to be used by their closest neighbor. They used the land and put a portion of the profit aside for Emile. He had never touched it.

But the house—the house and the barn stood empty. It was as if everyone knew that it was too sad a place to live in any longer but too sacred to destroy. The home Emile was born in, had grown in, and had died in. His breath caught in his throat as the car came to a stop, dust from the road creating a hazy atmosphere as Emile opened the door and stepped out.

It felt surreal. Birds chirped in the massive oak tree that shaded Emile's childhood home. The tire swing still hung from the branches, and it moved lightly in the soft breeze. Someone had trimmed the grass around the building as if they had known Emile was coming, but he suspected the neighbors did so out of respect and in memory of his family.

He heard Ash exit the car but at the same time he didn't.

He'd never known how he'd feel returning to his home. He thought maybe he'd be angry, or numb, or overcome with grief. But as he stood there, waves of emotions and memories washed over him, and he couldn't place a name on any of them.

"How do you feel?" Ash asked tentatively.

"I think I feel *everything*," Emile replied. "You know," he said, gesturing to the growing fields, "I thought I'd be upset to see the farm being worked. I thought it'd make me feel like nothing happened and no one cared. But it's so weird, because in a way, it makes me feel like . . . they're still alive. Like that day didn't completely destroy everything." A lump formed in Emile's throat and his eyes began to sting. It was now or never. He took a step forward and then another and briskly crossed the dirt path leading to his old home. He marched up the steps to the wooden porch, past the wooden beams, and walked across the threshold.

The soft light of a fading sun filtered through the window, flooding the living room in delicate hues of golden remembrance. It was just an empty house now; the furniture and belongings had been donated years and years ago. But Emile stood in the quiet capsule of his past, remembering each placement. His dad's easy chair facing the fire, the worn-out sofa his sister used to walk across, the rug strewn with toys and books that his mom was always asking them to pick up. His eyes swept from the left to the right, to the open kitchen where his mom had so often been found baking sweet treats or chatting over tea or coffee with her friends. He saw the ceramic-tiled kitchen table that Ash had his first family meal at, the flickering lamp that his dad had never been able to fix, the bookshelf his dad had made to house Emile's favorite books.

He saw everything and he felt everything. And for the first time in ten years, Emile cried. He cried for the little boy who didn't know what was to come, for the sister who would never live her life, for the parents who wouldn't grow old in easy chairs, for the life he should have had and never would. He sank to the ground, on hands and knees, his body racked by earth-swallowing sobs. He clutched his chest where his heart felt as though it would burst, and he stayed that way until there was nothing left but a stained wooden floor and a broken heart.

He pulled himself to the kitchen island and leaned against it, facing the living room fireplace where they had spent so much time as a family.

Finally, he rose and walked past the kitchen, past the reading nook with the built-in window seat where he'd spent hours devouring his favorite fiction of heroes and adventure, and down the hallway to their bedrooms. His sister's room was painted a light sky blue, decorated in wispy clouds and trees.

"We'll put some fairies in as she gets older," his mom had said, her arm wrapped around his shoulder. "She deserves to have a little magic in her world." And over the years, fairies, gnomes, flowers, and mushrooms had popped up in various places around the room, making it feel like a forgotten little magic kingdom.

"Everybody pretends they never existed," his mom had said as she painted the last fairy. "I was fourteen when the war ended. It had started well before I was born, but I remember spending my childhood moving from place to place, trying to outrun the bombs and hunts. My mom worked hard to keep me safe from the carnage, but I still saw the demolished towns, and I heard the stories of families torn apart because someone in their family had special abilities or sympathized with blessed beings."

Emile had loved watching her paint. It was soothing to watch his mother mix colors and turn a blank wall into something beautiful.

He shut the door and opened his parents' across the hall. Their room was painted a soft sage, his mom's favorite color. Across the wall by the window frame, she had marked Emile's and his sister's birthdays and heights. He walked over and ran his hand down the inked scribblings and saw Ash's name inked in next to his own. He smiled a half smile, remembering how his mother had fussed over Ash when he had finally warmed up to them and how hard she had tried to make him feel like he was a part of their family. His hand stopped at the last marking of his sister. At eight years old she'd been tall for her age, but Emile couldn't help but notice how small her markings were compared to his own. Ash had grown fast and surpassed Emile within a year—a full-grown man's body while Emile stayed long limbed and awkward. Ash had explained that was what happened to vampires. Elites grew at a remarkable rate, becoming full adults in just a few years. Turned carried that trait, developing into a fully matured body, fit for ultimate survival. Ash had been afraid he would scare Emile's little sister, but instead, she was sure she was going to marry Ash someday.

Emile let his hand drop and turned, memories of his parents' happy laughter and their whispered arguments circling through his head. His mom and dad had always been an affectionate pair—kisses on cheeks and lips, hand holding and hugging, and the occasional slap on the behind from his dad. They loved passionately and weren't ashamed to show their affection in front of their neighbors or their children. But Emile knew they didn't always get along. He'd heard the late-night arguing behind closed doors, but that was where it always seemed to stay. They never talked bad about each other, and they gave each other a chance to say what they needed to even if the other didn't agree. They had raised their children the same way—love passionately and listen actively.

He closed the door to their room and headed to his own. He paused as his fingertips touched the doorknob and then resolved himself and opened it. He was surprised to see a table in the middle of the room with several boxes on top. He walked over, opened them, and was once again overwhelmed as he saw his favorite books, his sister's stuffed toys, his mom's favorite tea cups. He pulled them out one by one and came across an old shoe box. He opened it and found pictures of his family. They had never been good at taking pictures, always busy, always forgetting. Many of them were impromptu with half of them looking away from the camera or doing something else, unaware of the photographer. Emile sifted through and saw there were also clippings about the farm, articles about gardening his mom had written, grocery lists, harvest schedules, receipts, and crayon drawings he and his sister had drawn.

Mom always said she had a special filing system, Emile thought. He placed the other objects back into the boxes and took the shoebox of memories back out to the living room. Ash was now sitting on the floor with his back on the kitchen island, but no cigarette this time.

As if he knew he said, "Never in the house. Mom would be so mad."

Emile chuckled and sat down next to him. "That's very true." They sat silently together before he asked, "Do you think they're watching us from somewhere?"

"I like to think so," Ash replied. "There's something beautiful about that idea—that there's something waiting for you after this life and that the ones you love aren't gone forever."

"Ash," Emile said slowly. "When you came to live with us, you left your old family behind."

"For the most part," Ash replied gruffly. "You never quite leave your family. There's always pieces that hold on to you."

"But you had sisters," Emile replied. "They were older than mine but still younger than you. I guess I never thought about it, but it must have been hard for you. To leave them."

Ash was quiet. "I didn't lose them like you lost yours," he replied. "When my parents sold me into the blood ring, I was glad to do it to keep my sisters safe, and the money my parents made from my feedings gave them a good life. I just didn't count on a vampire overdosing on me and killing me. And then bringing me back. They called my parents to me after it happened. They brought my sisters and they saw me change. And my youngest one cried, so scared of what was happening.

"'We have too many mouths to feed,' my father said. 'We don't want him back. If he dies, so be it.' So they left. And when I tried to come back, they didn't want to have anything to do with me. Not my parents. Not my sisters. I don't blame my sisters," he continued. "They only knew what they were taught, and they were taught to survive. I do blame my parents though. They shouldn't have had children if they couldn't take care of them, and I would rather have not been born than to have lived and witnessed all that I have."

"Don't say that. I wouldn't have survived if it weren't for you," Emile countered.

Ash looked at Emile, his face and eyes so sad Emile's heart dropped. Ash's eyes glistened and there was almost a look of desperation in them. Emile thought he had pushed too hard, so he quickly changed the subject and handed Ash the shoebox.

"It's Mom's filing system," he said jokingly. "Did you pick out all those things to save?"

"Yes," Ash replied, taking and opening the box. "When you didn't want to come back I tried to pick out things that would have the most sentimental value. I thought maybe one day you'd regret not having anything, so I put some aside when the neighbors cleared the house out."

He sorted through the papers and pulled out a pencil drawing Emile had made of a flying dragon. "Gods you were a bad artist," he said, holding the picture out and examining it back and forth.

"Better than you'd ever be," Emile replied, snatching the drawing away. "Do you think there are any dragons in Moon City?"

"I have no idea what's in Moon City," Ash replied. "But I think dragons ceased to be a long, long time ago."

"Yeah, maybe," Emile replied. He stayed thoughtful for a moment before he said, "My mom always hoped that magical beings would find a way back into the world. Vampire and human history were such a huge part of the start of it that I think people forget all the other beings that disappeared along the way. They really started disappearing long before that, the war just permanently took them out."

"That's what war is: beings who think they're right fighting against beings who also think they're right. Desecration and destruction in the name of belief. Don't get me wrong, sometimes there are terrible beings that need to be taken out, but the majority of us just want to live our shitty lives in peace and die doing what we love. Sixty years later and we're still reeling from it. Empty playgrounds, houses and populations decimated, and millions dead."

"My parents grew up during the last stretch of the war. Sometimes my mom would tell me stories about it. They really worked so incredibly hard to build a life, a good life, and raise good kids."

"And they did," Ash replied.

"I don't know if I'm good," Emile said. "I don't know anything about myself or what I want or what I should be, or . . . if they'd be proud of me. If my father saw me today, would he be proud of who I turned out to be? Or would he not even recognize me?"

"Of course he'd be proud of you. They both would be. Emile, you chose to live, and you chose to make the world a better place."

"By fighting the very thing I am!"

"By fighting the bad version of what you are. So what if you don't know who you are? Find out."

"I don't know how to do that."

"Emile, are you happy in Squall? Do you feel like you're serving a purpose?"

Emile paused, pondering his answer. "Yes. I mean kind of. Yes, I'm happy I just . . . I just feel like I'm going through life drifting along and following everyone else. I feel lost."

"I know what that feels like. I know you think I don't but I do."

Emile sighed. "Sitting here in this house just reminds me of who I could have been."

"And who is that?" Ash asked.

Emile thought for a moment. "I don't know. But now I'll never know!"

Ash tilted his head. "Maybe not. But if you keep holding on to that, you are absolutely never going to find out who you are now. You have to let it go."

Emile contemplated as he gazed at a family photo. He remembered the scene behind the picture. It had been a light spring day, and they were planting peach trees in their backyard. It was one of the last photos that they had taken together as a family. His dad was leaning on a shovel watching his mom tamp down the tree. She was busy laughing, her head thrown back, her brown hair dancing in the wind. His sister stood in between them, holding the twiggy tree and looking up at their mom. Emile could only see half her face, but it was wide and smiling. And finally, Emile himself was standing next to his dad, his mouth in a half laugh, watching the scene unfold. Ash had been the one behind the camera, having snatched it from Charlotte who had been taking random shots of flowers and birds. Emile didn't remember what they were laughing about, but it was a perfect snapshot of time. He slipped it into his vest pocket. This was one memory he'd be taking with him.

"Do you want to see where they are buried?" Ash asked quietly.

"Yes. Yes, I do."

The boys walked out of the house, Emile locking and closing the door behind him. He would leave the belongings of his family for another time. For the next time he came to visit them. He followed Ash off the porch and to the right, walking down past the barn. The barn too was empty, and they walked by the window of Ash's old room.

"That's empty too," Ash remarked as they walked.

Behind the barn was a pond that the kids had played in on hot summer days. Beyond the barn, at the tree line, was a meadow that grew soft grass and wildflowers. And there, under a massive weeping willow, lay three graves. The headstones were simple with their names, dates of birth, and date of death. The grass and flowers had long grown over the graves, making them indistinguishable from the rest of the meadow. The moon was fully out, casting a soft glow in the tiny graveyard, and both Ash and Emile stood silent, listening to the frogs singing from the pond.

"This was a really good spot," Emile replied, a mist gathering in the corners of his eyes.

"I tried to do good by them," Ash replied. "I'm so sorry I wasn't there Emile. I'm so sorry. If I had been there, it could have been so different." The words began spilling out of Ash, as though he couldn't control himself. "When I got here it was too late. Your parents... It was just carnage everywhere. And then there you were, barely breathing, and I couldn't believe you were alive! And your sister..." He trailed off.

"Ash," Emile said softly.

"Emile, I looked for her, I tried to find her before it was too late. I tried to track them down. As soon as I knew you were okay, I left for her. I searched for days until I finally got word that her body had been found and buried next to your parents. I tried, Emile, I tried. I'm so sorry..."

"It wasn't your fault," Emile interjected. "None of this was your fault."

"You don't understand," Ash replied desperately. At that moment, both of their pockets buzzed. Emile checked his device.

"It's Foxxe. He wants to know how much longer we will be before meeting them in Gardovia."

Ash wiped his face. "I'll take care of it. You should have a few moments with them before we go." He turned abruptly and walked back to the house, leaving Emile to say his goodbyes.

Emile suddenly felt awkward, unsure of what to say. He shifted from foot to foot, glancing up to the moon hovering in the sky. He breathed out a sigh and let his hands fall to his sides, hanging his head.

"I'm sorry I never came to say goodbye," he finally said. "The truth is I don't remember much from that day, just random flashes that make my head hurt. I don't know what happened to you. I don't know why it happened. I just know I woke up and you didn't. And I'm so sorry."

Emile began to cry softly, and he let the tears fall without wiping them away. "I have felt so guilty and resentful because I'm alive and you're not. And if I'm honest, I feel guilty because I'm glad I don't remember. I'm afraid that if I do, I won't be able to take it, or that I made a mistake, or that I didn't fight back as much as I could. They took you, Charlotte, and I don't even know what they did to you. I don't know how you died. I can only hope it was quick and painless. I'm sorry I wasn't there to protect you. I was your big brother, and I should have been there." Clouds were gathering in the sky, and a cool wind stirred the willow branches, but Emile ignored it and continued.

"I've been drifting along since you all died, I just couldn't accept it. I didn't know what to do, and when I tried to find your murderers no one would listen, no one would speak because an elite was involved, and no one will speak out against them. So, I just . . . gave up. And I've spent my life wishing I was a kid again and you all were alive still. I am so, so lost and I don't know what to do about it. I don't know how to live my life without you. I don't know what to do. I don't know what to do!" he cried.

"I just want you to be proud of me. But I keep thinking that if you saw me all you'd see was your killer, not your son. And that's what I do now, I kill things. And I'm good at it. Killing things is so easy. But living? When I woke up turned I sliced myself up hundreds of times in a million different ways because I was so angry that I was alive. Ash was the only one there for me who forced me to live and gave me a purpose.

"So I'm here now," he continued. "I'm here now because I don't know what to do and I don't know how to deal with this. But I have to try. I want my life to mean something. And I want you to be proud. I just want you to be proud of me. I'm sorry I didn't come sooner, but I promise you, I've thought about you every single day. And I still will, but it's got to be in a different way."

He wiped the tears from his eyes and face and took a deep breath. "I promise you; I'll find a way to make this world better. To keep this from happening to someone else's family. Maybe everyone else tiptoes around the elites but I will not—not anymore. I want my life to mean something, and I want your deaths to mean something. I don't want you reduced to some senseless slaughter. I want you to be remembered as people who inspired change."

He heard their vehicle start and he knew Ash was subtly telling him it was time to go.

"I have to go now," Emile said. "But I promise I'll come back to visit. I won't let whoever did this take that away from me. I love you all so much. You gave me a great childhood and a happy life. And I hope to gods you knew that up until the very last moment."

Emile closed his eyes and breathed out. "I don't know what the hell I'm doing. But I promise I won't waste another minute of this life. I am who I am because of who you raised me to be. Because of who I choose to be. And I choose to be your son. I choose to be your son." Emile placed his hand over his heart and closed his eyes as he repeated it once more:

"I choose to be your son. I choose to be *me*."

A light rain began to fall, twinkling the pond behind him and softening the earth before him. It began to soak his hair and clothes, rolling down his arms and face, but he didn't turn away, he didn't try to wipe it. Instead, he stood and let the water run over him as he did the rolling emotions within, the raw fullness of a heart carrying ten years' worth of grief and regret. Emile didn't stop the waves, he let them come, he let them overwhelm, he let them exist. He let go and allowed himself to be whatever he was going to be, and Emile felt in his bones that he would leave this place transformed once again.

Chapter Twelve

"Behold the blessings of the gods
Crimson deliverance from the curse of mortals..."

Gardovia was located in a wintery pine forest in the north of the upper district. Thick with blue spruce and green pines, surrounded by rolling mountains and dense shrubbery, it was a calm and quiet break from Lordestowne. The actual town of Gardovia was softly nestled in a valley between two snowy peaks. Gardovia was the kind of place you went to rest and live the remainder of your days, quietly. It was also one of the few places where vampires and humans lived together openly and peaceably. Many were descendants from the war, and their children played in the streets without fear. Snowmen dotted the road as Ash and Emile drove through to the local inn. Such harmony. And it was this reason that the forests of Gardovia housed a magical secret: the doorway to Moon City, the last haven for magical and unnatural creatures. It sat deep in the forest, far removed from the village, and the vampires of the town guarded their home and the civilians within it fiercely.

"Places like this don't feel real," Emile commented. "We live in a vampire-only community and the human cities I've been too feel incredibly foreign." He gestured. "Here they have peace. How on earth did that happen?"

"Because they came from war and loss. And taught their children better," Ash replied, pulling up to the curb. "I wonder if the others have arrived."

As if in answer, a shrill laugh pierced the frostbitten air.

"Oh Sam, you are *too* much!" Violetta stepped out of the inn with the district leader, Sam Wallace. Wallace was another elite vampire who worked with Foxxe in blight containment. He smiled at Violetta, flashing white teeth against his ruddy complexion, abashedly combing a hand through his sandy-brown hair.

Ash rolled his eyes and groaned.

"You could just, you know, express yourself so things like this don't happen," Emile pointed out.

Ash just glared at him.

"Oh, that's right. Feelings don't go with the rugged, 'I'm a mysterious loner aesthetic,'" Emile countered. He rubbed his chin thoughtfully. "Does 'pathetic loser' fit in there because that's the real vibe I'm getting."

Ash punched him in the arm before they both climbed out. Sam and Violetta were still casually chatting as the pair walked up.

"Ash, Emile! So good to see you!" Sam greeted, shaking their hands and pulling them each into a half hug. "Foxxe said you would be here soon!"

Though an elite, Sam was a younger one and Emile knew he felt more relaxed with the three of them. When around Foxxe and Annora, Sam assumed a much sterner countenance and leader-like presence. But when it was just the four of them, they felt like young adults who just wanted to have a good time. Emile had fond memories of their group hanging out late into the night, Sam getting a little too tipsy on some spiked blood and blessing them with off-key, lovestruck karaoke. It was the only time Emile had ever seen Violetta soften as she had leaned into Ash, the two of them silent, as though blending into one. But nothing had come from it, and the next day they had separated back into the roles of bloodthirsty vamps for hire.

"It's great to see you, Sam!" Emile replied. "Pity there's no time for a night out. Maybe next time?"

"Next time for sure!" Sam replied.

"And no spiked Nutrimentum for you," Ash teased, smiling around his cigarette.

Sam blushed. "Only in moderation."

"Well of course," Violetta replied. "Just a little." She winked and Emile swore she glanced at Ash as she did so.

The fond reunion was interrupted as Foxxe and Annora exited the inn as well.

"Good, now that we're all here we can begin our trek. I trust you've all taken the proper precautions heading out into the snow?"

They nodded. Since painful sensations were dulled in a vampire to allow for more endurance, burns, cuts, or in this case, frostbite, could lead to a more extreme wound. Although their self-healing was significantly increased, a wound that was not addressed or protected took longer to come back from. And where they were going, they needed to be on high alert and in full control of themselves.

"Sam's going to accompany us to the entrance."

Violetta, Ash, and Emile grinned.

"But there will be no partying along the way," Foxxe continued with a knowing look.

"Don't worry, Foxxe. You'll always have our best behavior," Emile replied.

Annora raised an eyebrow and looked at them skeptically. "I don't know that any of you have 'best behavior.' We just have 'somewhat listens'"—

pointing to Violetta and Emile—"and 'does what they want anyway'"—pointing to Ash.

"Annora, I am offended," Emile replied, feigning hurt.

Violetta laughed, as did Ash.

"Oh!" Emile replied indignantly. "I see how it is. Fine. You two can walk together then. I'll walk with Sam. I'm sick of looking at your toothy grins."

And with a wicked smile at Ash, Emile locked arms with Sam and continued back into the inn, spying Violetta wink at Ash, pricking her tongue with a fang.

"I've got all your rooms ready," Sam told Emile. "You, me, and Ash will have one room, the ladies another, and Foxxe has his usual room at the end of the hall. I asked if he wanted to join us, but he said he didn't want to crash our time together. Or argue over who gets the cot."

"Emile gets the cot!" Ash yelled from the back.

"Not if I get there first!" Emile yelled back. Sam grinned and together they bounded up the stairway.

The inn was old, a call back to homey village days. The walls were painted a dark green trimmed in cream. It felt warm and inviting with old paintings on the walls and homemade quilts on the beds. A crackling fire met them in their room, two twin beds to the right of the fireplace and a cot placed cozily in front. A massive window to the left brought in a view of the pine-scented forest and snowbanks.

"Back home there is no snow," Emile commented. "We're just getting colored leaves actually."

"Snow always arrives early here," Sam replied. "It's because we are so far north."

Emile walked over to the beds and threw himself on the one closest to the fire just as Ash burst through the door.

"Well, well, well. Guess you're a little late," Emile taunted, his arms behind his head as he wriggled in his bed.

Ash threw his pack onto the other bed. "Not that I can see. Sam didn't claim it so it's mine now."

Sam laughed. "That's fine with me. You're guests here anyway. Besides, the cot is right by the fire. I will be the coziest of all of you. No, no, it's too late, don't try and swindle me. You had your chance at this strategically placed, luxurious cot. It is your loss!" And with that he dramatically flung himself across it, lying languidly by the fire.

"So dramatic," Ash replied. "I see you haven't changed much."

"Dramatic? I don't know what you're talking about," Sam replied cheekily, propping his hands under his face. "And talk about changing, still smoking, are we? Better not let the lady of the inn catch you. She'll have your hide for smoking in here!"

"Well thank gods for the window," Ash replied, strutting over to the massive glass. He flung it open, and a gust of wind wafted into the room. Emile thought of another time when such a gust would have made him shiver. But he lay in bed, unfazed by the cold. The lack of sensation was something he'd never gotten used to. Probably never would.

"Ugh, this room reeks of testosterone already," Violetta announced, leaning against the doorway.

"I thought that was your favorite?" Ash remarked, puffing away.

"Not when it's laced in cigarettes and sadness," she retorted. "See you guys later, I'm going to freshen up for dinner."

"She means take a nap and try not to think about me," Ash clarified.

"Go to hell, Ash," Violetta called, walking away.

"Are you two . . .?" Sam questioned.

"No, but they should be," Emile replied for Ash.

Sam widened his eyes and smiled. "I always got the impression it was heading that way. Violetta can be a little unpredictable with those knives she loves so much, but she always seemed comfortable with you, Ash. She still does."

Ash chuckled and tossed his butt out the window. "Crazy likes crazy," was all he replied.

Emile supposed that was true considering the company he kept. He supposed they were all a little crazy in some ways. The boys reminisced and joked as they rested before dinner.

They gathered together in the inn's dining room, crowded around a rectangular table with a few others from Sam's squadron.

Violetta had indeed freshened up, bedecked in her favorite purple and black-laced corset, her perfect curls framing a sultry face. Emile caught the look she gave Ash as she walked in, sitting down beside Sam. His eyes narrowed as he switched his gaze to Ash who simply leaned back in his chair, arm slung over the back carelessly while he smiled and cocked his eyebrow. But Violetta turned her attention to Sam, and Ash rolled his eyes to the vampire sitting next to him, listening to him regale her with a story of their latest blight kill.

The conversation was light as everyone drank their Nutrimentum and caught up on the latest gossips between the districts. This was one of Emile's favorite parts of his job—seeing the different districts and the way people led their lives. Gardovia was so very different from Emile's home. It wasn't just the atmosphere or the small village, he realized, it was something much deeper. It was the absence of fear. The absence of fear and the complete ease that both humans and vampires coexisted in. Emile wondered if the qualities of Gardovia could be extended to the outside world, where media and government fearmongers stoked hatred between species. He thought of Link's city and wondered if City Salvatore could become a new Gardovia. He thought if anyone could make that happen, it would surely be Link.

After dinner, the table was cleared and shared reports spread across it. Blights weren't just a problem in Emile's hometown. It was a widespread occurrence. Between the spontaneous blights and the uncontrollable rogues, both human and vampire, all the squadrons were being kept remarkably busy.

"It's like they're being dropped off," Sam said, pointing to the infestations his squadron had taken out. "Absolutely no sign, not even an inkling, and then all of the sudden—mass attacks. And all the spontaneous ones have been hard to take out. They've been massive, strong, fast. Far more endurant than what we are used to."

"Have you lost any of your squadron to them?" Foxxe asked.

Sam's face clouded. "Yeah, a couple. But not always from the blight."

Annora's eyes narrowed. "What do you mean?"

"I mean we'll be fighting blights and some of my men mysteriously go missing," he replied. "Completely vanished, no bodies, no blood. Just gone."

"Deserters?" Ash asked cautiously.

"Never," Sam replied vehemently. "Everyone in my company is here of their own choice, and they are free to go at any time."

"Elites or turned?" Foxxe asked.

"Both," Sam replied. "I don't know what's happening, and we can't find them anywhere. I've reached out to other squadrons, and they're experiencing the same thing. Vampires and even humans just gone from their squadrons and towns."

"I've gotten the same reports," Foxxe replied. "Anyone missing here in Gardovia?"

"No, the town has remained secure. I don't think anyone is particularly interested in our quaint little village. And anyone going to and from Moon City knows to keep a wide berth. But when we aren't hunting blights, we're hunting rogues. There's been an uptick in both human and vamp rebels breaking into cities, smashing up blood banks, and harassing the public. It's been overwhelming!"

Foxxe leaned back in his chair as conversation flowed across the table. Emile could tell there were a million thoughts racing though his brain. Foxxe glanced at Annora and they shared a look as though swapping information. But neither spoke and Foxxe closed his eyes.

"We're going to Moon City," he finally said, "because I've heard that some of the elites are defecting from the vampire capital. I want to know why. There are two currently camping out in the city, so my company and I are going to pay a little visit. There's been disruption in the vampire factions for years now, and I would not be surprised to learn that the elites are behind this. And if my suspicions are confirmed, I need to know who will be willing to stand against them. I think all the rogue activity has been a distraction for something much, much bigger."

Silence fell across the table. Emile knew the weight of those words. To stand against the elites would mean a war between the vampires. A war they wouldn't all come back from.

"We will stand with you always," Sam replied steadily. "We've seen the warnings on the horizon. When the time comes, Foxxe, we will be there to back you up." His companions nodded solemnly. "And I know the other district leaders will as well."

"I hate to ask this of anyone," Foxxe said, slightly slumping against the back of his chair.

"I know," Sam replied. "But you're not asking. We're volunteering." A cheer went around the table and Foxxe smiled.

"Take some time to enjoy yourselves, everyone," Annora said, rising. "We'll be departing at ten tonight to get to the entrance on time. Please be ready to leave, we must stay on track since the doorway is only visible for a short amount of time."

Sam took Ash, Emile, Violetta, and his companions on a brief tour around the town and stopped in at the local pub. They didn't stay long, just enough to bid Sam's company good luck, and then the four of them headed back to the inn.

They trucked up the stairs to the boys' room and sprawled out, relaxed. Violetta was perched on Ash's bed, idly polishing one of her many knives while Ash casually observed from the bay window, cigarette softly smoldering. They murmured quietly so as not to disturb the floating music coming from the record player in Foxxe's room.

"Does he often keep to himself?" Sam asked. "He always did when I worked under him, but I thought it might be different with you lot."

"He likes giving us space," Violetta remarked. "But yes, Vaughn Foxxe is a quiet soul who enjoys his solitude."

"But he'd be there for us if we needed it," Emile interjected and Violetta nodded. "He gave Ash and I a place to stay and a job. Said he saw something of himself in us. Told us we could be more than what we'd come from if we wanted it."

"Annora said the same to me," Violetta mused. "She had to do a little convincing to get Foxxe on board, but it wasn't too bad."

"Do you think you all might lead your own company someday?" Sam asked.

"I don't know," Emile replied slowly. "I can't imagine not being in Squall. We all work really well together. We're kind of a family," he added.

"Gag," Violetta commented. "So emotional."

"Oh come on, you love us," Emile retorted.

Ash looked at his cigarette and flicked the glowing butt out of the window.

"Love is overrated," she replied casually.

"Only with the wrong people," Ash said quietly from his perch at the window.

Violetta rolled her eyes but didn't reply, instead turning her full attention to the blade in her hand.

"Maybe we will have a new company someday," Emile ventured. "You never know what could happen."

Ash looked at Emile, a curious look on his face. Emile just shrugged and looked away. He wasn't ready to have that conversation with Ash. He was still afraid of what Ash might have to say. Or not say.

The fire crackled peacefully, and Emile wished for a moment that it could stay like this. That life would pause in this quiet, snowy town, that Sam could stay and laugh with them, and they could all just exist for a little while—free from purpose.

"Awful quiet in here for such young and ambitious vampires," Annora called from the doorway. Her black hair was pulled back in a ponytail, a long braid trailing her back. She was dressed in a warm turtleneck sweater and thick black leggings that hugged her curves. A wide black belt decked in daggers set up her hourglass figure. A freshly polished glaive swung from her belt, gleaming in the firelight. She tugged at the dagger popping out of her thigh-high black leather boots. "Are you ready for Moon City?"

Emile had never been to Moon City. He'd only heard stories about the mystical town. They trekked through the forest quietly and at a steady pace, light snow falling. It glittered in the moonlight, coating the trees in a radiant kind of splendor. At the end of the war, many of the nonhuman beings lived in fear of another purge so they created for themselves a little pocket free from the human world. Only those deemed unnatural to the human world were allowed in, and the doorway to Moon City could only be seen during the witching hour, when the spirit realm blended with the living realm and the power of mystics and science was at its peak.

Just as Emile felt he couldn't walk another step, Foxxe halted the company. He motioned them forward, stepped between two massive pines, and seemed to disappear. The company followed one by one. Emile held his breath and took his step, followed by Sam. The snow disappeared and they found themselves in a glen coated with soft grass and blooming flowers. In the middle were two stone pillars engraved with magical runes. And between the pillars was a shimmering arched doorway—into the heart of Moon City. The company stood before it, the luminescent light bouncing off their faces.

"All right, Squall," Foxxe said. "Remember: stay together and don't divert. This may be a place for those like ourselves, but it doesn't mean it's safe. Do not engage with the locals and don't eat or drink anything given to you. Single file please. Remember our objective."

"Well this is where I say goodbye," Sam said cheerily, clapping Emile on the shoulder. "Don't have too much fun in there."

"Have you been?" Emile asked curiously.

"Once. It's an interesting place. You'll see."

"We'll see you after though," Ash said, securing his pack.

"Oh for sure," Sam replied. "My squad is close by in the area, so I'll be meeting up with them, and then I'll be back to escort you back to the town."

"How will you know when we're back?" Emile asked.

Sam held up a small round object. "A beeper! We have sensors here so we know when folks are coming in and out of the city."

"Clever," Ash remarked.

"We'll see you, Sam," Emile replied. "Don't miss us too much."

Sam laughed and the company made their way through the door to Moon City. Emile had walked through magical barriers before thanks to Sean and the Sentimental Dead, but this was totally different. For a moment, Emile felt a slight tickle and then an itch, as though he needed to sneeze, and badly. But then he blinked, and they were standing on the other side.

People hustled through the streets before them, not sparing a glance at the group that had come through. Emile called them people but what he saw was an assortment of witches, wolfhounds, warlocks, and various other nonhuman entities.

They thrummed through the streets, some posted at street corners selling magical brews or rare ingredients. Some stood casually sharing conversation with one another. Emile was dumbfounded—never in his life had he ever imagined a world where strange and unusual beings lived and thrived. Beside him, he heard Ash and Violetta exclaiming their own surprise. The city was incredible and undeniably beautiful.

Foxxe led his company through the lamplit city and down the cobblestone streets. Moon City looked like something out of a fairy tale—colorful buildings in strange shapes that defied gravity and physics, curious trees growing golden fruit, floating starlight lanterns that twinkled silver stardust, music floating devoid of cacophony. It was indeed magical.

Beneath the fairy-tale exterior there was a sinister shadow to the bright colors. They passed a gated cemetery with a "Dig a grave for a fee—no questions asked" sign. Along the way, Emile saw various blood bargaining shops, turned for hire stations, shops selling love potions and hexes, and most popular, the Witches Transformation Den. Witches skilled in the art of transformation made a pretty penny changing appearances for a fee. In another life they could have been highly valued plastic surgeons, but here in the safety of Moon City, innocents and criminals alike could erase their identities and start over. The elites Foxxe had come to talk to were on the list of the witches' customers. Emile wondered how Foxxe had come across that information, but Foxxe had his ways, a million intelligence stations that Squall would probably never know. He'd seen a small glimpse into that with Branswick and Stylos.

They made their way through the town, the band sticking close together. The atmosphere became darker as they passed creatures making deals in alleyways, skimpily dressed young women beckoning on the corners, and drunken beings preparing to brawl in the streets.

They rounded the bend and came up to a tavern. Boisterous music echoed from within. The tavern had seen better days, the outside a bit faded and shabby, its sign swinging in the wind, squeaking on its rusted chains. Inside dingy lights lit the booths and tables. To the left of the entrance, a ragtag group of musicians played a low-key melody, adding to the hazy atmosphere. Across from the band, several bartenders worked, mixing drinks and chatting up the customers sprawled across the bar. In one of the booths, tensions flared and weapons were drawn, silencing the room. Foxxe halted and the band stood still before the weaponed table let out a laugh and resumed their business. The band resumed playing and everyone continued on as though nothing had occurred.

Emile pulled himself in, avoiding bumping into the host of bodies swarming the area. Across the way at a lone table lounged two males. They had been idly stirring their drinks and sprang to attention at the sight of Foxxe. Emile and his associates slid into the circular booth on each side, blocking the exits and trapping the elites in their spot.

"Foxxe," said the dark-haired male. "What a pleasant surprise." His voice practically dripped with sarcasm.

"Likewise, Renalt. Stenson." Foxxe nodded to his companion.

"And what brings the almighty Squall to Moon City?" Stenson asked, his teeth glinting in the murky light. "Didn't think this was the sort of place you would subject yourself to."

"Well, when I heard that two of the highest guards in the elites had defected, I simply had to find out why."

The two vampires exchanged uneasy looks.

"That's why you're here," Foxxe continued casually. "Looking to get a makeover and start fresh. Seems a bit rash considering the plush lives guardsmen like yourselves are afforded. Must be something awful to make you leave."

"We don't know what you're talking about," Renalt said darkly.

"And it'd be a shame if your captain discovered you were here. If someone had a finger on a button that would alert them immediately. If I were you, I'd do what I needed to in order to make certain that didn't happen. Can't even imagine the punishments that'd be awaiting my return."

"You're bluffing," Stenson retorted, his eyes piqued with fear.

"You know who I am," Foxxe replied. "How much is your life worth?"

The chatter and clamor of the bar circled around them.

"And if you think about causing a scene," Foxxe added, "just remember where you are. Victory goes to the most prepared. I came prepared." He gestured to his companions. "And I'm not afraid to pay for damages. But you two probably have your money invested in your transformation. I wonder. Two against five and no money to boot."

"Just say what you want, Foxxe," Renalt grumbled, swirling his glass. "We're on a schedule and would like to be on our way."

"Interesting," Foxxe replied. "Most folks have to wait months for a transformation. You have to pay a pretty penny to get to the top of the list without notice. Must have taken you a bit to save up. Just how long have you been planning your departure?"

"Close to a year," Stenson replied. "Back when our people started disappearing."

Foxxe inclined his head, asking him to continue.

Renalt sighed. "Surely you've had reports of vampires gone missing? Seemingly vanishing in a moment? It isn't just happening to your precious squadrons. It's happening in our ranks too."

"And why?" Foxxe asked.

"You know that as elites it's our duty to further our bloodline," Renalt continued. "And to promote strong and healthy descendants. It started with the isolation and removal of those elites and turned deemed weak, liabilities, nonessentials."

"And who deems them nonessential?" Annora inquired.

"The clan lord," Stenson answered. "It started out as a strongest and fittest trained and rewarded. But then vampires began disappearing, and he said it was a cleansing and part of the natural order of things. Then he evolved and began using it to take out anyone who dissented. But not publicly. Quietly. In the dead of night, on a patrol, wherever they could be taken without notice. They were labeled as deserters and defectors."

"Which you are," Foxxe pointed out. "Kind of stands against you. So how do you know this?"

"Because they took my wife," Renalt growled. He crumbled only slightly before reinforcing his iron wall. "They took her when I was out on a patrol. But

I returned early, see, and they weren't expecting that. They had her tied and gagged, dragging her out of our home by her hair. I tried to fight them, but they cited her for questioning the clan lord, and as the wife of their high guard, she needed to be made an example of. So, they held me down as they slit her throat. Inflicting wounds so she couldn't heal, couldn't repair. And when she died, they left her body there and told me to do my duty. We had been planning on leaving. We should have left as soon as it all started."

"So you left after that?" Foxxe replied.

"Not right away," Stenson answered. "We continued on as though nothing had happened, waiting for an opportunity to disappear on an assignment—get a head start before anyone realized we were gone. But more and more of us disappeared. There were murmurings of a laboratory beneath the clan lord's chambers. You could walk the halls and hear muffled screams, as though it was haunted."

"And then the flooding of the blights began," Renalt pointed out.

"So you believe the clan lord is responsible for the blights?" Foxxe questioned. "You think he's abducting vampires and altering them into these creatures? Why?"

"Wouldn't you know better than us, *commander*," Renalt sneered. "Been gone a long time but you still ought to know better than the rest of us. He's waiting for you, you know. Don't you wonder why there's been so many rogues going wild all of a sudden? Kind of a nice distraction, don't you think?"

Emile turned a quizzical eye to Foxxe, but Foxxe kept a steady eye contact with Renalt.

"So you finally left," he said. "Any specific reason why now? Or were you just next on the list?"

"Get your shit together, Foxxe," Renalt spat. "Because there's going to be a war on your hands. The clan lord has completely lost control. There's chaos and division riddled in our factions. Our people are going missing. You would do well to look after yours. And if you do go home, be prepared not to come back."

Foxxe paused thoughtfully. "Would you stay and fight?" he asked. "Would you stay if there was a revolt and a new order brought to the clan?"

They both shook their head. "I have nothing left to fight for," Renalt replied. "I could not care less what happens. I want to live out the rest of my life in peace."

"And where he goes, I go," Stenson replied. "He is as a brother to me. I will not abandon him."

"Then we will leave you to your transformation," Foxxe said as he rose. Emile and the rest of the company also stood, relieving themselves of the table.

"For what it's worth," Foxxe said softly, "I am sorry about your wife."

Renalt simply raised his glass before slumping into his chair.

"Good luck, Foxxe," Stenson replied. "You will need it. *Even unto the ends of the earth.*"

"*Even unto the darkness which must always descend,*" Foxxe replied bitterly.

Emile had only ever heard Foxxe utter this exchange with other elites from the vampire country. It was a sacred tongue, an ancient text that didn't belong to the turned. Not that Emile particularly wanted a part of it.

Foxxe led the company out, and Emile took one look back at the two vampires. He felt a mixture of pity and disgust as they walked away.

Chapter Thirteen

"Cast off the names given of the womb

And embrace the divine..."

The End Is Nigh

They exited the bar and Emile assumed they'd be on their way out of Moon City. He was eager to see what was next in store after their conversations with Renalt and Stenson. Surely they had enough information to make an active move on the elites. The rogues, the blights, they were all connected. They all came back to the same source.

A few streets down from the bar, however, Foxxe took a detour on their way out and stopped at a turned for hire station. Turned vamps who were abandoned by the elites or had chosen to go on their own path often ended up doing hired work. Some of it was perfectly legit—escorting people through territories, doing muscle work, working security at events—and some of it wasn't, like rogue work or blood trafficking.

"I'll be right back. I have something I need to attend to." He disappeared into the station leaving the rest of them outside. The streets were crowded, and Emile and Ash stood to one side of the entrance as Annora and Violetta drifted to the other. Emile couldn't explain it, but he felt a coldness begin to creep over him as they stood in the alley.

"I'm pretty sure that we're being watched," Emile whispered to Ash.

"Yeah, I feel that too," Ash replied lighting a cigarette. He casually scanned the crowd, nonchalantly taking a drag. "Do you see anything?"

Emile took in the crowd trying not to appear too obvious. "I don't know. Something just doesn't feel right."

As he turned away from Ash, he felt cold hands on the back of his neck.

"Hey, sweetie," a sultry voice purred. "You're looking a little lonely."

Emile jerked back from the woman sidling up to him. She was shorter than Emile, curvy, with silky red hair combed away from her face. She removed her hands from Emile's back and instead coyly threaded them through his arms.

"My name is Maggie. What's your name, handsome?"

Emile untangled himself gently and replied, "I am so sorry but I am not lonely. Thank you though, uh, but no."

"Hmmm." Maggie frowned. "That's okay. How about your friend? He looks like he could use . . . some relief."

She walked over to Ash but he pulled away. "I'm sorry, Maggie, but I'm afraid neither of us are interested tonight."

"Oh, are you together? I don't mind that at all." She licked her lips slowly. "There's plenty to go around."

"No, we are not together," Emile replied quickly.

"Well then I don't see what the problem is," Maggie answered. "You don't have to be shy. I'm very affordable and . . . discreet." She playfully pushed her breasts together before dropping them and letting them bounce.

Emile noticed that the streets were getting busier. A warlock rushing through pushed against Maggie, knocking her into Emile. He caught her and helped her stand, blushing as his hands brushed against her breasts.

"It's the killing time," Maggie announced, fixing her attire. "Everyone's on their way to the games."

"The killing time?" Ash asked.

"Yes, the time of day when the drunks are at their drunkest and brawls are at their deadliest. Everyone heads down to this side of town to place bets on which brawler will come out alive."

"Seems a bit violent," Ash commented.

"You're not from around here, are you?" Maggie asked, surveying them. "You were new faces to me, but people are in and out of here all the time."

"No, we're not from around here," Ash replied.

Maggie looked at them suspiciously. "You new turned for hires?"

Emile and Ash glanced at each other. "Yes," Emile replied. "We're new."

"Uh-huh," Maggie answered skeptically. She turned to continue on her way. "Be careful here, boys. This isn't the place for unseasoned turneds. And stay away from the killing time. They like new blood." She disappeared into the crowd immediately, almost as if she hadn't been there to begin with.

"Violetta!" Annora's voice rang out over the crowd. "Violetta! *Violetta!*" she screamed desperately.

She ran to Emile and Ash, her eyes wide in panic. Emile had never seen her this distraught before, and it frightened him.

"Someone took Violetta!"

"What?!" Ash choked, grabbing Annora by the arms. "What do you mean someone took her?"

"The crowd swelled, people were yelling. A couple of drunks barreled through and knocked me down, and before I even got a chance to get up, Violetta was gone! Come on, we need to find her!"

The three of them broke apart, pushing through the crowd and calling for Violetta. They received no answers, only rude stares and questioning looks. Emile could hear Ash screaming.

"Get the fuck out of my way!" He cursed. "Violetta! Violetta where are you?"

"Emile!" A voice rang out. "Emile, what is going on?" Foxxe appeared next to Emile and pulled him out of the fray.

"Annora said someone took Violetta. We split up to look for her, but we didn't see where she went."

Foxxe's face went ashen. "Let's get the others." He pulled Emile behind him as he ducked into the street. They moved as swiftly as they could catching Annora and then Ash.

"We need to go," Foxxe said.

"We need to find Violetta!" Ash argued.

"You won't find her here," Foxxe replied.

"How do you know that?" demanded Ash. "We could be wasting time right now."

"Because of this." Foxxe held up a cream-colored note with one line, stamped with a red seal:

"It's time to come home. She'll be waiting for

you."

Annora snatched the paper, her hands slightly trembling. "I know this seal," she whispered. She quickly turned to Foxxe. "They have her, don't they?" Tears threatened to spill from her dark eyes.

"They do," Foxxe replied. "And we are going to go get her."

"What the actual fuck is going on?" Ash demanded, distraught.

"The elites took Violetta. They've been trying to get my attention for months now. I guess they decided to take a more brash approach. I didn't think they would risk taking one of my squadron. But they did, and now they will pay. So, we're going to go meet them as they have requested."

"Where are we going?" Emile asked.

Foxxe turned and Emile took a step back at the anger simmering in his eyes.

"Home."

Chapter Fourteen

"Bare your fangs, a mark of transformation

Holy, holy are we..."

The last twenty-four hours had been a blur. Emile and company had rushed out of Moon City, meeting up with Sam. Sam had told there there had been an entry and an exit after Squall had entered the city, but he had not thought anything of it as beings were always coming and going, and he was devastated to hear that Violetta had been part of the exit. They did not stay in Gardovia that night. They packed their things, said goodbye, and hurried on their way.

To the elites. To vampire country—*true* vampire country. The territories that Emile was used to were largely populated by turned with a few elites sprinkled here and there, but where they were going was the elite homeland.

"Home."

Foxxe's word echoed in Emile's head. Of course, he knew that Foxxe was an elite, but it had never occurred to him that Foxxe may have lived there at some point. For the entire time that Emile had known and worked with Foxxe, he was the opposite of everything that elites seemed to stand for. It was odd to think of a young Foxxe dwelling in vampire country. It made Emile realize just how little he knew of Foxxe and where he had come from. It had never seemed to matter though because Foxxe didn't carry himself like a typical elite. Like he was better than everyone else. And yet. He still was one.

And Violetta. Emile felt a lump in his stomach as he thought of her separated from them. He couldn't bear to think of her as yet another missing being when so many had vanished and never returned.

Across from him in the vehicle, Ash sat silently, his knee bouncing uncontrollably. For the first time in a long while, no cigarette hung between his lips. Emile had only ever seen him like this one other time, when he had woken from his fevers and completed his change. Thunder raged in Ash's eyes and Emile knew there was carnage and bloodshed on the horizon.

Foxxe and Annora sat in the front of the vehicle, Annora at the wheel and keeping a steady pace. There were bouts of conversation and then silence. They swapped their knowledge of the elite station. Annora had been there more recently than Foxxe, having been born and raised there many years after Foxxe had departed. She told him what she could recall in terms of layout, and Foxxe in turn shared his, things both from his past and from the sources he had scattered throughout.

"There's something you need to know before we get there," Foxxe said abruptly. He twisted in his seat to look at Emile and Ash.

Ash's knee bouncing came to a halt and he pulled himself away from the window and leaned forward. He looked ages older. Emile supposed love, even unspoken, would do that to a person.

"I was born in the beginning, when vampires were first starting to emerge," Foxxe began tentatively. "Far enough in that elites had started forming their own communities, but still in the days when vampire babes and their mothers were being slaughtered. It was a dark time to be born."

"My mother was just a young thing, married off to the local butcher much too early, and burdened with child not long afterward. The pregnancy . . . was not normal, obviously. She began exhibiting symptoms of a vampire pregnancy—an insatiable craving for raw meat, extreme pallor and unnatural weight loss, nightmares, sleepwalking, and sharper senses. The town surmised that what she was carrying was a demon. Her husband was convinced she had slept with the devil."

Emile shuffled uneasily in his seat. Annora had told him about those dark days but hearing it from his leader was unnerving. He glanced at Ash, but Ash merely sat silent. Focused.

"And since he was the local butcher," Foxxe continued. "He decided that the only lawful thing to do was to cut me from my mother's womb. What he did not anticipate was that my mother loved me, and there is nothing in this world quite like a mother's love. She fled in the middle of the night and sought asylum in the nearest vampire colony. Keep in mind, back then vampires did not live openly, and our existence was equated with that of demons and monsters, so for her to run straight into the bowels of a human-perceived hell was incredibly brave on her part."

"The vampires confirmed the presence of an elite pregnancy and sent her to the place all mothers now went—to the clan lord. He offered her protection both while pregnant and after. All of her needs would be met, and she would be allowed to remain with me as I grew. It sounded like a dream for a woman destined to be butchered like a common farm animal, but the protection of the clan lord came with a price. Experimental procedures and testing as well as forever remaining on vampire soil, and she was never to return to her family or human civilization. But, as I said, my mother loved me, and she would not leave me. And so, I was born."

He paused for a moment, the weight of his history hanging on his brow. Emile wondered at the vampire before him—one of the originals, one that almost never was.

"The clan lord took an interest in me as I grew. He felt there was something special about my existence, including the fact that my mother had bonded so fiercely with me when so many other mothers rejected their vampiric offspring. He was present in my schooling, chose special activities for me to be involved in, and began grooming me for a leadership position from a very young age. The first hundred years of my life were spent under his direct tutelage. He taught me the art of war, the power in persuasion and seduction of my enemies, how to play every mind game and how to outwit every opponent. There was nothing I could not do by the time he was satisfied. He was hard on me, but he challenged me to grow. He challenged me to be more, always."

"You sound as though you care for him," Ash said sarcastically.

"I did," Foxxe replied. "He was like a father to me, and I only wanted to make him proud. I wanted to be worth the special attention he gave me. I wanted to be a leader. My early days were spent leading his rebellion, teaching his doctrine, fighting his wars. I did not know any different." He sighed before continuing. "You see, boys, this place isn't just my home because I was born there. It is my home because it is my birthright. It is my claim. It is the place I was born in and the place I am destined to lead."

Emile held his breath as Foxxe finished.

"I am the adopted son of the clan lord. His position is to be mine. These lands belong to me."

Emile felt rocked to his core. He had always known that Foxxe was an elite—but this? This was too much to take in, considering all the events leading up to this moment.

"And yet you're here, leading Squall," Ash replied, jolting Emile. "A dedicated and loyal servant to the human race and an honorable and well-respected war hero to the masses. What changed you, Foxxe?"

"My mother," Foxxe said quietly. "The abuse that my mother was subjected to was hidden from me at great lengths. Her frailty and health issues were attributed to her weak human deficiency. There were times I was not allowed to see her, and the clan lord would tell me she just needed rest and quiet and that my presence was too much for her at times. My mother never said a word, and I did not know any better. She died when she was only twenty-nine. A thin, broken woman who looked like she had lived a thousand lifetimes, in none of which she ever knew love or care. But I did not know—how could I? At that point I was still fresh blood and had never left vampire country. But I hated that humanity had crippled and destroyed my mother. She had never wanted to be turned, and I did not know until much later that she was not allowed to be. I will never know what her real choice would have been, if she would have stayed with me forever.

"But as more and more mothers came to vampire country, the facility housing them grew. I had never had any interest in visiting. It reminded me of my mother, and I had no wish to revisit that sadness. But right around the age of 125, things had begun to change drastically in the vampire house. The clan lord had begun collecting wives, some human and some turned. And that's how we found the first blight. He was punishing her and denying her food and she began the change. Instead of getting her help, he locked her away as his personal experiment and watched her slowly morph into a hideous creature. It was terrible. And it was then I began to see him in a new way. A much darker way.

"I decided to visit the place where my mother had lived most of her life, and what I found there was shocking. Electrocution, starvation, sensory deprivation, water tanks where the women were submerged for copious amounts of time to monitor body changes and brain patterns. Women chained to their beds because they tried to leave. Women locked in rooms, screaming in birth with no one to assist them. It was absolutely horrific. It was then that I found my own mother's file and the lengthy experiments she had been subjected to in her short life. It broke my heart.

"This was the cruel side of the clan lord that I had never seen. The facade began to crumble as I began looking in places I had never been allowed. I stole away to the human world and walked among them and saw not the frail, worthless beings I had been taught existed. No. I saw beauty and creativity. Hope and promise. Resilience unlike anything I had ever seen. And I saw love in a way I didn't know existed. Not the love that I knew—love that was earned. Love that was taken away in the face of disappointment. Love that was pain and loss. I looked at this world, and I realized that I couldn't fight for my father anymore. And whatever love I had for him crumbled to nothing. By that point, there was a war brewing. I joined the other elites and turned who had fallen from vampire country. I kept myself anonymous for as long as possible, knowing they would never accept or trust the clan lord's son. I fought with them, and I used every tactic my father taught me, and we *won.* The very few who knew where I came from accepted me, and I became the leader my father always wanted to be. Just not for him. Never for him.

"I have spent my life trying to undo the things he has done. I know it's probably hard for you to accept—maybe you feel disillusioned or betrayed. I understand. But I would hope the years and service behind me speaks more than my family. I have worked hard for what I have, and I have never stopped."

"Why have you not tried to unseat him?" Emile asked.

"I have. Many times. But he is strong and influential, and he has his own government of loyalists who serve him. I cannot undo a monarchy in a lifetime, let alone a day. But the tides are changing and things are not what they were. Now is our time. To rescue Violetta. To stop the spread of blights. To end his tyrannical and terrible reign."

"You have never failed us, Foxxe," Emile interjected. "You are the bravest and most honorable elite I know. We are lucky to fight alongside you. Where you came from doesn't matter," he said, a heaviness lifting from his chest. "All that matters is what you've done since. And it's damn impressive."

Foxxe nodded, his face solemn but filled with relief.

"How many people know who you really are?" Ash asked, curiously.

"Annora, Stylos, and you two," Foxxe answered. "A couple others who fell in battle."

"Well, gods!" Emile exclaimed. "I guess we are pretty special."

"Kindly keep the specialness to yourself," Foxxe interjected.

Emile and Ash nodded.

"Okay," Ash said next. "What's the plan?"

Chapter Fifteen

"Oh sisters, oh brothers, go forth now and multiply
Even unto the ends of the earth..."

The Past Isn't All Dead

The plan was simple. There would be no sneaking, stalking, or secrecy as they entered the city. Squall would walk right in the proverbial front door. Foxxe felt there was no need for stealth—the elites knew they were coming. They were expected.

"She'll be waiting for you."

As they rode toward the vampire capitol, the sky grew dark and ominous, a storm rolling in on the horizon. Fitting. The weather matched the tone.

Emile could tell when they entered the elites' home, and he had never quite seen a town like this. The houses were painted in dark plums and grays and were connected together via tunnels and shaded bridges. Annora kept an even acceleration as they traversed worn brick roads winding their way to the center. There was not a vampire in sight, and Emile wondered if they were all waiting for Squall to arrive. Would they leave this place? The thought sat heavy on him. He was startled out of it as the vampire capitol came into view. Emile hadn't been sure what he was expecting. He'd heard plenty of stories of the ancient vampire home, but it didn't prepare him for the magnificence in person. He leaned forward; his eyes wide.

"Vampire elites are nothing if not dramatic." Foxxe sighed as the top came into view.

It was majestic. Built in the style of an old Gothic cathedral, it was decked in beautiful stained-glass windows and wore a crown of twisting spires, formidable gargoyles, and sweeping archways. It was terrifying and beautiful. As they approached, Emile noticed that the covered bridges and tunnels all led to the cathedral. Castle? Emile wasn't sure what it was technically called besides an intimidating fortress filled with fangs and certain doom.

Annora pulled up to the impressive structure, its shadow looming over them in the dying light of a clouded sun. Each member opened their door and stepped out into a mist. The stone stairway led to massive iron doors framed by weeping stone maidens. The four stood together, feeling the energy pulsating around them. It was quiet. But not the quiet of a sunset. The quiet of an impending storm.

Foxxe nodded to them briefly before straightening his shoulders and leading the way. They strode up the steps, the clicks of their heels the only sound penetrating the silence. Above the door was inscribed a passage from the ancient vampire text:

"Go forth now and multiply
Even unto the ends of the earth
Even unto the darkness which must always
descend."

Emile paused to read it briefly before sprinting to the front doors beside Ash. They opening the heavy iron and wood passageway for Foxxe as he strode through.

They opened into a giant sanctuary, the stained-glass windows seen from afar framing the entire room. It would have been church-like, holy even, were it not for the stone pillars lining the way to a single throne where sat an ancient-looking man. The clan lord. Emile felt ice in his veins looking at one of the oldest, if not the oldest, elites in the entire world.

"My son," he said, rising from his seat, black robes spilling around him. "You have finally returned home to me." Beside him stepped forward his guards, tense and ready to fight.

Foxxe stopped about twenty feet from the elder and faced him.

"Hello, father." Bitterness and regret coated the words as they hung in the space between them.

"You don't sound happy to see me," the clan lord said. "But I see you brought your new family. Do they love you, Vaughn? Do they love you the way that I do?"

"Better," Foxxe replied. "This is my company, Squall. Annora Winters, Ash Crosse, and Emile Thorne. But I suppose you already know all of that."

"I do, yes," answered the clan lord indulgently. "I know them all very well."

"Well, then I suppose I should introduce them to you," continued Foxxe. "Friends, this is Ascelin Vesper, the clan lord of the elites."

"And of the turned." Ascelin gestured impatiently. "People tend to leave that part out."

"Enough of this," Ash interjected brashly. "Where is Violetta?"

"Oh, your final companion. Dreadfully spiteful I'm afraid. She put up quite a fight on the way here. And afterward." Ascelin shook his head disappointedly. "She would have made a fine soldier here in our capitol. What a waste."

"Where. Is. She?" repeated Ash.

Ascelin smiled, as though placating a temper-tantrum-ridden child. "She's here. Well, she's down below actually. Since she couldn't be reasoned with, I'm afraid we had to chain her up. But don't worry, she is a fantastic specimen. Perfect for the next stage in our experiment."

Foxxe held a hand up in front of Ash, signaling him to be still.

"Give her back," Foxxe replied. "Return her to us and we will leave quietly."

"You can go and fetch her if you so desire," Ascelin said, waving to a door to the side. "But you may not want to unchain her."

Ash bolted to the door, Emile behind him.

"In a hurry to prevent the loss of another loved one are we, Ash?" Ascelin interjected, not moving from the place he stood. "Did you run this fast when you heard what was happening to Emile's family?"

Ash stopped in a dead halt, his back to the rest of them. Emile saw his shoulders sag beneath his navy coat.

"Don't listen to him, Ash," Emile said. He reached out to the door as Ascelin spoke again.

"Oh, I see. Emile doesn't know. I always wondered about that."

Emile's hand wrapped around the door handle as an unnerving sense of dread settled into his chest.

"I can't blame you for never telling him, Ash. Though, I wonder, did you see them every time you looked at Emile? How do you handle the guilt knowing you're the reason his family was slaughtered? How do you handle *him*?"

Emile slowly turned to look at Ash, his best friend, his brother, the one person in the whole world who had always been there, who had always protected him.

"Ash?"

Ash stood silent, his face downcast and dark, bathed in shadows. "I didn't know, Emile. I didn't know," he muttered. Ash rubbed his face violently, digging his fingers into his forehead. "It was an accident."

"What are you talking about?" Emile asked in almost a whisper.

"Why, the death of your family," Ascelin answered. "It was because of Ash. You see, Ash still felt responsible for that regrettable family of his. Leftover human emotions are so . . . unpredictable. So he got back into the same business he died in. Blood prostitution. Except this time, he was ferrying humans to us in exchange for the safety and well-being of his family. Things got out of hand though when Ash caught a conscience—*morals* if you will."

Valkane's words flashed in Emile's mind, and his body trembled as the words spilled from his lips: "You brought them to us."

"It wasn't supposed to happen," Ash answered desperately. "Yes, I did go back to it for a while. I thought maybe I could at least get my sisters back. I just wanted them to be safe! But nothing I did was good enough. They didn't want anything to do with me. Your dad caught me, he didn't even condemn me, he just tried to talk me out of it. And it worked, and I left, for good."

Tears brimmed in Emile's eyes, his body locked in anger and rage.

"The vamp I was working for threatened to come after me for quitting before our contract was done. But at that time Lordestowne was in a power struggle, and he was killed. I thought we were safe. We were, for a long time. The attack came out of nowhere. I didn't know they were coming, Emile. I didn't know!"

"You knew this, all this time, and you didn't tell me?" Emile screamed.

"How could I?" Ash screamed back. "You were dying! Changing! You were so unstable I couldn't even leave you alone for a moment without coming back to a flayed-up corpse to be!"

"I deserved to know!" Emile countered. "All these years I have been left in the dark, not knowing how they died or who did it. But you knew! You fucking knew!"

"I can't change it!" Ash yelled. "I would if I could. In a heartbeat. I would have rather died than your family. You think I haven't suffered this whole time knowing, knowing I have betrayed you every time I even look at you? The least I could fucking do was keep you alive and make sure you had a life, no matter how much you hated it. You had to stay alive—YOU HAVE TO STAY ALIVE!" He panted. "Violetta isn't dead—she's down there waiting for us. I can't save your family, I will never be on time for them. Please let me be on time for her," he begged.

"When this is over"—Emile spoke callously—"you will never speak to me again. I will never have anything to do with you again."

Anguish rippled across Ash's face, but he simply nodded and dashed through the door.

"So dramatic," Ascelin said sarcastically. "Such grief for a family that's not even dead. Well, not completely dead."

Emile turned slowly and took a few steps toward the elder vampire.

"What the fuck are you talking about?"

"Emile, we need to keep focused," Foxxe interjected.

"Oh, but I'm having fun," Ascelin pouted sarcastically. "We're only just getting started. Let me show you what I've been up to. What I did to bring you home to me."

He snapped his fingers and the ruby curtain behind him dropped to the floor. Bound and on his knees was Admiral Rawlings, the ill-mannered man who had insulted them in front of Commander Hoyt. But he looked different this time. He looked . . . feral.

"Try to make some allies with humans and they get greedy," Ascelin said. "They start threatening you with violence and guns and bombs as if they are the supreme power in the world. So predictable. So annoying. They wear out their usefulness. No matter, we found a new use for our admiral. First, we turned him. And we let him get very, very hungry. And then"—Ascelin removed a syringe from his pocket—"we dose him." He strode briskly forward, plunging the syringe into the admiral's neck, making the feral man scream beneath his gag. Ascelin stepped back, satisfied.

"Father." Foxxe sounded broken. "What have you done?"

"Something transformative," Ascelin answered, opening his arms. "A new age of vampire power has arrived my son. Nothing can stop us. We are the supreme power."

As he finished speaking, the admiral fell to the ground, seizing and spasming in violent bursts. His limbs began twisting and breaking, reforming into extra limbs with long claws. Emile had never seen a transformation before and, based on the looks of Foxxe and Annora, neither had they—at least not one like this.

What was once the admiral was now mutating into a giant, lumbering beast, arms and legs stabilizing the gigantean form. A large, beating black heart was framed in an impressive ribcage. This one would be difficult.

Ascelin beamed proudly. "Blights have always been so unpredictable. You never know what size or shape you're going to get. But now we've perfected it. Massive creatures. Magnificent."

The blight roared, shaking the walls and floor, deafening the room. More guards swooped down from the ceiling, winding the massive creature in chains attached to bolts on the floor.

"You can't control them," Annora interjected.

"We don't need to," Ascelin replied. "We only need to drop them off. Discreetly. With the help of a few insiders. Like this one was. Until he got just a little too greedy."

Emile felt the rage return, remembering Captain Hoyt's lifeless body hanging between the teeth of a blight much like this one. Brought to the compound by the admiral. How very fitting that he himself became one.

"And it was easy getting test subjects," Ascelin continued. "Traitors that didn't understand the importance of establishing our rightful place. I think you met two of them. What was their names? Oh yes, Stenson and . . . oh, I forget the other. Doesn't matter they were failures in the long run. We tested them right after they gave you the prompting to come home. It didn't take."

"Did you learn nothing from the war? From losing our people? From losing me?" Foxxe asked angrily.

"Obviously," Ascelin answered. "I learned that humans bring out weakness in elites and turned alike. It is time to start over by erasing turned creations and ending the overpopulation of human spawn."

"I won't let you do this," Foxxe said, drawing his weapons as Annora followed suit.

"You don't have a choice," Ascelin replied and waved his hands to the guards. "You never did."

The guards leaped into action, deftly moving against Foxxe and Annora. Emile moved toward them, but Foxxe called him to stop.

"Wait," Foxxe commanded, slitting the throat of the first guard. He turned to his father. "What did you mean his family isn't dead?"

"Such trivialities, everyone will be dead soon anyway," Ascelin replied, turning away and shrugging.

"Indulge me," Foxxe countered, decapitating a second guard.

"Very well." Ascelin turned, annoyed, and looked Emile up and down. "Your sister is alive."

Chapter Sixteen

"Even unto the darkness

Which must always descend..."

Emile had to remind himself to breathe as the weight of Ascelin's words hit his chest. His sister—alive? Charlotte was out there, waiting for him.

"Where is she?" Emile demanded.

At that moment, the blight, which had been struggling against its imprisonment, morphed a second mouth on its belly. The mouth was filled with sharp, jagged teeth that broke through the chains almost instantly. With a ferocious growl, it descended on four claws and began grabbing the guards in reach, feeding both its gaping mouths.

Emile joined Foxxe and Annora as they stepped back from the carnage. One by one, the guards were swooped up to waiting teeth, and the blight was soon coated in a sticky, red hue. The few remaining vampires ran from the blight, leaving Ascelin alone and unprotected.

"Come away from the beast!" Foxxe yelled.

"Nonsense, this is my child," Ascelin cooed, looking fondly at the abomination.

As if in reply, the blight leaned down on all its legs and arms, leveling itself with the floor, gazing into the eyes of its creator.

"Now, now, no need to act like that. I'll take you where there is plenty of space and lovely humans that taste ever so delicious."

The blight sat quietly for a moment, as though contemplating Ascelin's words. Ascelin slowly reached out his hand, caressing the gray, decaying flesh. It was almost a tender moment.

Until the blight morphed another mouth atop its head and snapped the fresh jagged teeth just above Ascelin's waist. He was snapped right in half, his legs being chewed by the hungry monster.

Foxxe ran forward, followed closely by Annora as the blight chewed and swallowed Ascelin's lower half. It stumbled backward, claws scraping at the flesh of its body, slicing away folds of skin.

"I don't think you agree with him," Foxxe observed.

"He doesn't agree with anyone," Annora pointed out.

"He overfed." Ascelin gasped, blood streaming down his chin. "He didn't have time to stabilize."

They watched the blight continue to claw its body, stumbling backward and crashing through one of the walls, the ceiling and bricks burying it. It shrieked, attempting to stand, only further pulling debris onto itself until it gave one final breath, its body buried and silent.

The silence brought with it cries and shouts from multiple points in the vampire community. Emile looked at Foxxe quizzically and Foxxe smiled. "Sam, Stylos, and several other companies didn't want to miss out."

Foxxe stood to leave, and Ascelin grabbed his hand.

"Son," he gasped. "This is your birthright, it is time to claim what is yours."

Foxxe looked at him sadly. "This is always what you wanted."

"I loved you, always." Ascelin choked.

"I know," Foxxe whispered. "And I loved you once."

Ascelin continued choking and sputtering on the blood, smiling at Foxxe before finally lying still. It was over.

"Help!" Ash's voice rang out in desperation as he fell back through the door carrying Violetta. Violetta clung to his chest, panting and trembling, terrible mutations appearing and then disappearing on her skin.

"They dosed her, micro doses," Ash explained. "We have to help her. Please," he begged. "Please."

Tears streamed down his face in a way Emile had only seen once—when he'd first awoken from his change.

"I can take her," Annora answered, taking Violetta from Ash's arms. "There's a secret medical base that's been working on cures. If anyone can help her, it's them."

"Let me come with you," Ash pleaded.

"No, you have work to do here," Annora answered gesturing toward Emile. "And Foxxe will need your help as well. The world has ended, gentlemen. A new one is now beginning."

Annora tenderly gathered Violetta to her and kissed her forehead before departing down the steps. Within moments, the hum of the company vehicle could be heard speeding away.

Foxxe was now encompassed by various squadron leaders, including Sam and Stylos. Apparently, it had been a relatively easy take-over. But it wasn't done just yet. The plans and creations of Ascelin were spread far and wide. It wouldn't be easy bringing it all to an end.

And Charlotte. Charlotte was still alive.

Emile turned to Ash, who stood waiting for him to speak. He knew this person better than any other, and he saw him bracing for rejection and anger.

Emile didn't think he could ever forgive Ash. But he did have to talk to him.

"I don't want to speak to you," Emile said coldly.

"Okay . . ." Ash replied, narrowing his eyes.

"But I will for Charlotte," he continued.

Ash's eyes shot open. "Ch-Charlotte?!" he stuttered.

"Yes," Emile said as he turned away, walking toward the door. "Charlotte is alive and you're going to help me find her." He stopped, a new feeling settling over him. Certainty. Purpose. Darkness.

"And we're going to slaughter the ones who took her. Light a cigarette, Ash. We're going hunting."

Squall will return in

Book Two

of the

Sanguine Sorrow Trilogy...

Sacraments

In full transparency, I never actually believed this book would see the light of day. I kept plugging away at it, hoping I would make definitive progress, but life had alternative plans for me.

I had originally planned to release this novel in October of 2021 and even announced it on various social media early that year. My health took a turn for the worse, however, and in the spring of 2021, I was forced to undergo major surgery that has taken me over a year and a half to recover from. I had also already established and started running Curious Corvid by then. As my flock grew, my time diminished, and I was forced to sideline my own work for the time being.

It sounds sad but I'm honestly so happy that I was forced to wait. I ended up changing my story and had the incredible opportunity to work with the ever-talented Mark Alexander McClish on the beautiful cover art. He is also responsible for the weathered pages. Mark really brought my story to life with his art, and it was worth the wait to see this transformation.

Transformation is a heavy theme throughout my life. We are all in a continuous cycle of change and transformation be it for better or for worse. I have learned that while most change is not in our power, the aftermath is, and it is our choice and will that determine the ultimate outcome. I wanted that theme to come across heavily in my book and challenge the concept of "monster". I think change sometimes makes us *feel* like monsters. We have to relearn ourselves; we have to put up boundaries, we have to re-prioritize, and this transformation doesn't always sit well with the people around us. They may feel jealous, or angry, or even hurt. But as long as you are doing the very best you can with what you have, no more should be demanded of you.

I digress.

I thank my husband Link, who has sat through *countless* rants, explanations, divergencies, panic attacks, and blank stares as I processed life through a fried brain. I thank him for the late nights when I promised I was coming to bed but never did, for the hours he has spent picking up the slack so that I could create, for the patience he has had while I figured this whole thing out. I thank him for the unconditional love and acceptance he has always given me. I love you more than love, Link. In any galaxy, in any time, in any place. It is always you. *"Even unto the ends of the earth, even unto the darkness which must always descend."*

I mentioned him before, but I thank Mark Alexander McClish for making incredible artwork and being a loyal and passionate partner in Curious Corvid. His art made me feel like a real author and sparked the excitement that had been previously overshadowed by anxiety. Mark, you continuously amaze me, and you have given me so much hope. I can never thank you enough for the countless things you do for me and CCP on a daily basis. People like you make the world beautiful.

I thank Enoch "Stormy" Black for being a cheerleader and beta reader. Stormy followed my progress from the beginning and encouraged me to keep going. He comforted me when I was forced to delay and continued to ask questions about it along the way. Thank you, Stormy. I don't know if you realize how much that meant to me. I know there are amazing things of dragon-esque proportions waiting for you.

I thank Anna Corbeaux for being a brilliant and compassionate editor. I was so nervous to send her my novel. I felt so out of place, so awkward, so *trite*. But Anna brushed all those things aside and gave me confidence and a beautifully smoothed out book. Thank you, Anna, for being such a lovely person and incredible partner of Curious Corvid. You make our house that much brighter.

I thank each of my curious corvids both past and new. You all give me motivation to do and be better. Your bravery and boldness encourages the same in me. You give me direction in my chaos, and you give me a reason to compel my soul to carry on another day. I'm humbled by your faith and affection, and I hope that I always follow through and make you proud.

And I thank you, dear reader, for taking some time to get to know me and my little monsters. I hope you enjoyed them and even loved them. I will see you soon...

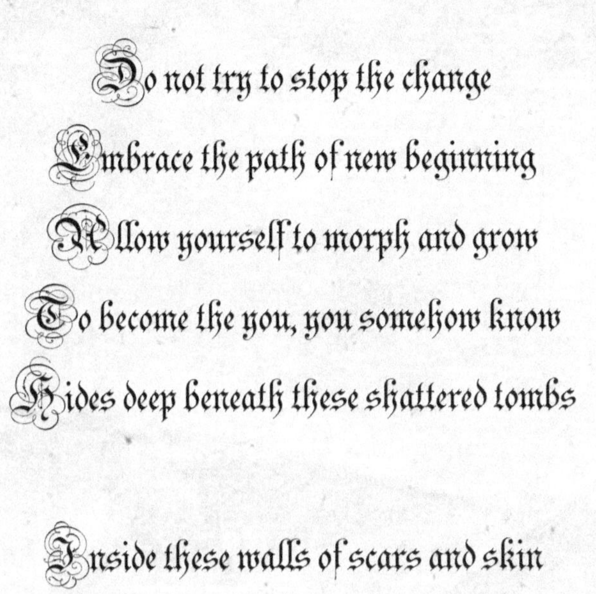

Do not try to stop the change

Embrace the path of new beginning

Allow yourself to morph and grow

To become the you, you somehow know

Hides deep beneath these shattered tombs

Inside these walls of scars and skin

Sleeps something waiting to begin

Comfort lies in pain and pleasure

Only you can make you better

More so now than once before

Intrigue is knocking upon your door

Now pass away this life you live

Good things are coming if you let them in...

Emile
Ash
Violetta
Foxxe
Annora
Enjoy...
281